The Volunteer

Other Titles by Nathan Everett

For Money or Mayhem

Computer forensics detective Dag Hamar is pulled from behind the safety of his computer and takes to the streets when he discovers a link between an online predator and real life kidnappings around Seattle. His fledgling romance is threatened when his girlfriend's daughter is suddenly among the missing.

For Blood or Money

Computer forensics detectives Dag Hamar and Deb Riley discover secret files and hidden code can be as dangerous as dark alleys and flying bullets as they track a missing man and the billion dollar fortune that went with him. Fourteen years after *For Money or Mayhem*.

The Gutenberg Rubric

Two rare book librarians race across three continents to find and preserve a legendary book printed by Johannes Gutenberg. Behind them, a trail of bombed libraries draws Homeland Security to launch a worldwide search for biblio-terrorists. Keith and Maddie find love along the way, but will they survive to enjoy it?

Steven George & The Dragon

Steven has always known he was a dragonslayer, but on the day his village sends him to slay the fearsome beast he realizes he doesn't know what a dragon looks like, where it lives, or how to kill it. His quest is facilitated by the exchange of "once-upon-a-times" with the people he meets on the endless road. Think Grimm. For young adults, not children.

The Volunteer

Nathan Everett

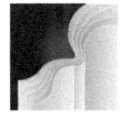

ELDER ROAD BOOKS
BELLEVUE, WA

*To my daughter who believes in me,
and to those who gave me courage.*

◆◆◆

A COLD WIND BLEW across G2's face and he stirred in his sleep. He clenched his eyes shut against wakefulness, but the ammonia smell of fresh urine assaulted him. He could have slept through the wind. He just never got used to the piss. He didn't think it was his, but his hand slipped down to his pants just to be sure.

G2 cracked one eye open. Wee Willy was still letting go with a gusher not ten feet away against a bush that was nearly dead from the frequent waterings. G2 should have put his bedroll further away.

Before he let go of the last vestiges of sleep, G2 assessed his situation as he did every time he awoke.

No. It didn't feel that way.

There was no "make you feel good inside" feeling. No deep satisfaction. No heroic pride. No nobility. None of the things there should have been.

When you read about it in school — back in sixth grade or so — you always knew the hero had that feeling. Like that Union soldier who led the charge up some hill in the history books. He knew when he set foot outside the bunker that he wouldn't make it halfway up the hill before forty musket balls peppered his body. But someone else would pick up the flag where he fell and move it further up the ridge. He knew he'd done his job — done his duty. He was brave and heroic and proud. He was satisfied that his life had meaning. He felt good inside, even while he was dying.

That was the way it was supposed to be when you volunteered, even if it meant you died in the process. You felt good about it.

Gerald Good, G2 to everyone else, checked again. He looked for the feeling. The satisfaction.

No. It didn't feel that way.

◆◆◆

BAD X was making his way through the camp, putting the touch on people to pay their "union dues." Bad X was an organizer. It seemed there was one in every camp. G2 considered slipping out of camp while Bad X shot the bull with Greaser. It wouldn't make a difference, though. Bad X would catch up with him tomorrow or the next day. You didn't want to get behind on your dues. Of course, G2 could hop across the track and catch the train for Cincinnati that was leaving the freight yard. G2 was pretty sure it was in Cincinnati that he met his first Bad X, though, so it wouldn't be any different there. Besides, if you didn't pay your dues to Bad X, you couldn't point to him when Bad Y or Bad Z showed up. You could always count on some bad ass coming around. You put the touch on folks at the supermarket and Bad X put the touch on you in the camp. Only most of the time you didn't beat the folks at the supermarket to a pulp.

Shit. He might as well be working at General Fucking Motors.

"G2, my man." Bad X grinned showing the empty spaces on either side of his one remaining front tooth. "Watcha got for me, brother?"

G2 reached out his hand and let his one crumpled up dollar bill fall out of it into Bad X's giant paw. It took a minute for Bad X to smooth out the bill enough to tell what it was.

"That all you got?" G2 reached in his pocket and produced another quarter. He nodded his head. The weight of his chin seemed to drag his head down to his chest. Maybe Bad X wouldn't beat him.

"When you gonna get your shit together, G2? Don't know what I'm gonna do with you." Bad X sat down on the upturned tin can next to G2 and slumped himself forward. From a distance they looked like identical statues — the kind of urban art you find at bus stops and random corners of public parks. "Brothers hearing the news" the artist would title the sculpture. People would read it and then walk all the way around the statue, trying to figure out what kind of bad news the brothers had just heard. "Death in the family," one would say. "War," would come from another. "Wall Street collapse," a third would chime in. Whatever it was, it had to be terrible. Two grown men sitting there as morosely as if the world just ended. Some guy in a wool scarf would come by and look at them. The sculpture would "speak to his heart." The next day he would come back with a friend and two more scarves. He'd wrap one around the neck of each of the bronze brothers and then sit beside them in the same position — chin lowered to his chest and shoulders slumped forward — while his buddy took a picture of them with his cellphone and posted it to Facebook. When they left, the guy in the scarf would consider leaving the scarves around the bronze necks for others to see, but then he'd grab them as he walked away.

"It's the 'conomy, stupid." Bad X chuckled at his joke. No one in the camp had ever got it. "You can't even get sober for a buck. You go MacD's and you still need the quarter to pay the tax on their dollar menu." Bad X tilted his head to consider G2. "You been panhandling down in the district?" G2 nodded slightly. "Those rich shits don't care about you. You gotta go to Safeway where moms with three kids hanging off their skirts will give you money to keep you away from their babies. They cover it up by trying to teach their brats about helping others. That's okay. You get down there and be an object-lesson to the little ones."

Having finished his lecture, Bad X stood up to move on. G2 didn't move.

"G2." He looked up. Bad X was holding the quarter out to him. G2 reached up for it slowly. "Bad X never leaves a man with nothing," he whistled through the gaps in his teeth. "Put some more with this and bring a bottle of two-buck chuck to my fire tonight. We'll call it even."

G2 watched him go. Looked like Whiskers would be the next one Bad X touched. He looked back. G2 picked up his canvas bag with "Windows XP" stenciled on the side of it and headed out to work the parking lot at Safeway.

◆◆◆

THERE WAS TOO MUCH TIME to think, that was the hell of it. When that kid in the Civil War — or was it the Revolution? — when he went charging up that ridge, he only had to hold his thoughts of honor and bravery for a couple of minutes before they cut him down. It was

3

over. He could spend eternity being a hero. Twenty years, though. That was too much time to think. That kid couldn't have held his self-satisfaction and good feelings for five minutes if the first bullet hadn't killed him. Twenty years going up the ridge — why that'd drive a man crazy. Had it only been twenty years? It seemed like forever.

G2 pulled the piece of church bulletin out of his pocket from last Easter. He had four of them stashed in his bag. He got them out of the recycle bin before the janitor chased him away. All the words to a hymn G2 didn't know were printed on one side. A lot of Jesus and halleluiah. But the other side was blank. It was clean pink paper. He couldn't understand why that rich church threw away perfectly good blank paper and then chased him away from taking it. Enough paper and you could do anything. One day he'd write all about what it was like — his life experiences. He'd sell the books to that rich church about how he was saved by the words of a hymn in their recycle bin. His experiences kind of all ran together after a while, though. He didn't know exactly where to start. But he had paper. He dug the stub of pencil out of his pocket and chewed a bit of the wood back away from the lead.

"XXN417," he wrote. Yes. That was definitely a good one. He hadn't seen a license plate with a higher number than that. It wouldn't be long now until he'd see one that started with "Y." Maybe two or three months, or when he got back next spring. He put away his pencil and paper. Wouldn't write down anymore today. It wasn't like he was obsessed with it. He just liked knowing what number they'd got up to. There was meaning to the order. He would figure it out eventually. He held up his cardboard sign and a driver at the exit rolled down the window.

"G2," the driver said. Well, of course he knew G2's handle. It was scrawled on his sign right under "God bless." G2 walked over to the car and bowed his head respectfully. "Have you eaten today?" G2 shook his head. "Here," said the driver. G2 held out his hand hoping for a dollar and the driver put a wrapped granola bar in it. "That'll give you a little something in your stomach."

"God bless," G2 whispered as he stepped back on the curb. The car pulled out of the parking lot onto 32nd Street and headed west. G2 put the bar in his canvas bag and waited for another car. Rule number one: Never let them see you eating.

Sometimes they were like that. They wouldn't give you money because that just encouraged panhandling and drunkenness. But they couldn't let you starve either. So they'd break into a six-pack of granola bars and give you one. Or they'd hand you a Jell-O Pudding Cup. Maybe they'd have a piece of beef jerky or half a sandwich. Stuff you had to eat today or it would give you cramps and the trots. They never cared about tomorrow. Why should he?

But when somebody gave you food, you never stood there and ate it. That discouraged anybody else from lending a hand. They'd see you had food and figure you weren't bad enough off to need their help. It was like people who only played the lottery if it was over 20 million. Enough to make it worthwhile. That was the problem when there was a line of cars. If one person gave you something, that let everyone else off the hook. So you stashed the bar, the sandwich, the yogurt in your bag and waited until enough cars passed that those in line hadn't seen you take a gift. Then maybe another one would feel generous and this time you'd get a buck. If you got enough... Well, five bucks would get you a liter-and-a-half bottle of cheap sweet wine. You could share that around the fire at night. Guys would give you their food for a taste of your wine. That was the way it worked. If G2 couldn't make a few more bucks today, he'd trade that granola bar for a drink of someone else's wine. G2 didn't mind. He could go two or three days without food before his gut started tying up in knots. Going without wine was a lot harder. It made him think too much. That thinking. That's what makes life miserable. If you just keep thinking about it, you'll go crazy

◆◆◆

THE LINE IN FRONT of the Job Corps office was long, as usual. Maybe even longer. G2 really couldn't think why he got up to come over here this morning They never had anything for him. He didn't think they even liked him. Mexicans would get all the good jobs before he even got to the door. The Chinese lady who asked for your name and identification definitely didn't like him. She got mad because he couldn't understand her. Apparently her Spanish was better than her English because the Mexicans all seemed to understand her just fine. They grinned and nodded their heads and then they went to work. G2 wasn't really sure if he would trust her enough to get in one of those trucks with the Mexicans, headed to some sort of job somewhere he didn't know doing something he didn't know how to do. He wouldn't put it past her to send him off to a concentration camp. Maybe he'd disappear and nobody would know he was gone until they got sent to "a job." They did that kind of thing. "What happened to G2?" Bad X would ask. Someone—maybe Bill White, black as night—would say, "I think he went to Cleveland. He been talking about Cleveland." Like G2 would ever go to Cleveland. It was too cold there to live on the street and G2 hated the shelters that made you listen to the preaching and made you take a shower while they kept your bag "safe" and wouldn't even let a bottle of cheap wine through the front door. He could stand the other if he could have a drop of wine. But no. It was like a concentration camp. If he got in one of those trucks to go to a job, he would disappear like a Jew in Poland and they'd dig his bones out of a mass grave in fifty years and say "Oh look. It's G2. Guess he didn't go to Cleveland after all."

Two men walked across the street and stood in line behind G2. They weren't day laborers. You could tell by their easy stance and the pack of cigarettes they shared. They must have come from across town to get the good jobs at the Job Corps. They were big men. G2 felt tiny standing in their shadow. He felt his heart beating faster. They would probably get nice clipboard jobs while G2 lifted boxes of fruit off a truck. That Chinese lady didn't like G2. But she'd like these two. She would treat them special. "You want to work in air conditioned place?" she'd say to them in her Asian accent. Chinese? Japanese? Some nese. "I got nice supervisor position just made for man like you." G2 just wished they wouldn't stand so close behind him. There was a whole sidewalk there and they didn't need to crowd him. G2 hated crowds. Crowds were dangerous. What was that story about people getting trampled in a football stadium? Or was it a nightclub? Didn't make a difference. It could have been in line at the Job Corps. Newspapers would have headlines in the morning. "Stampede at

Job Corps kills one, injures many more." Would he be the one or the many more? That's why he always put his bedroll on the far edge of a camp. Some people liked to be in the middle of things, surrounded by bums snoring and farting. You could die of ass-fixiation if you slept in the middle of camp. G2 had to get out of the middle. If he moved someone would be on him. Someone would step on him when they got up to take a leak. Some sloppy drunk would fall over him and then beat him up for being in the way. G2 didn't like having someone walking around while he slept. It wasn't natural. When G2 lay down on the outer edge of the camp, he could get up and leave whenever he wanted to. He might decide to catch that early morning train west and no one would be the wiser.

Gerald had once been in the middle of a crowd of cheering, happy people. How can people in a crowd be happy? It was in high school or college; he couldn't remember for sure which. When did he play ball? He played ball, didn't he? The team won a championship and people flooded onto the court. Everybody was hot and sweaty and stank. Not just the players. The whole crowd stank. Gerald had a sensitive nose. Crowds stank. He hadn't been the star player, but he played. He was caught up in the frenzy of cheering, back-slapping, and hugging. Hot stinking bodies gripping each other in big bear hugs like some orgy was happening. First the team and the cheerleaders. That was nice. Then the coaches and students and parents and teachers. Were his parents there? Gerald struggled to place them in the crowd, but they didn't materialize in his mind. They weren't always in Gerald's memories, so he must not have been very important to them. They weren't there to see him score in the last minute of the game and they weren't there in the crowd afterward. It wasn't the game-winning point. Their team was way ahead, but he scored. The crowd and teammates and cheerleaders were all there pushing around him and touching him. It was a happy time. How could a crowd be happy? G2 tried to find that feeling he had of joy and excitement that made being in a crowd okay. But he couldn't feel it. Even thinking about that crowded gymnasium with people pressing against him from every direction made his heart beat faster. And it wasn't happy. It felt like he couldn't breathe. He tried to find the excitement and joy, but only found panic.

G2 turned in the job line to ask the men to back off a little and let him breathe. Their smoke was choking him. Three more guys had joined the line behind them. Gerald stepped out of line. There were too many people standing there, waiting to get in trucks and be taken to concentration camps where they would be crowded into cattle cars and wouldn't be able to breathe. He motioned for the two big men with cigarettes to move up and take his place as he walked resolutely to the end of the line. They looked at him strangely, but moved up to take his place. G2 stood at the end of the line, almost gasping for air. He saw another man approaching from across the corner. Abruptly, G2 turned and walked away. There weren't any jobs there for him anyway. They didn't like him at the Job Corps. By the time he got to the front of the line, that 'nese woman would be sending people away, saying, "You should come earlier. Don't be so lazy." There just was no use being there.

♦♦♦

THE MANHATTAN CLUB was a business district café where the almost-there businessmen took their clients and secretaries for lunch. The real executives didn't go outside for lunch. G2 could imagine them sitting in their offices with secretaries feeding them some egg foo young prepared by their private chef. The Manhattan Club was for those who didn't have private chefs, but they looked like important people, anyway. When the important people wanted to be seen, they sat next to the big windows at the front of the restaurant and looked out on the street. Everybody ignored the businessmen who took their secretaries and mistresses to the enclosed booths at the back of the restaurant. Nobody ever looked at them as they went in, like only their waiter ever actually saw them. G2 worked there as a busboy once and got fired for looking at a man and woman in a booth. All he did was look and they fired him. Between the show-offs in the window seats and the non-existent people in the booths, there was the boisterous crowd around the oyster bar, slapping each other's backs and ordering another martini.

Bad X always told G2 he was wasting his time going to the business district. Executives didn't want to be seen giving money to bums. Executives wanted the streets cleaned up and people like G2 put in jail. That's what Bad X always said. If you spoke to an executive, just to ask for a damned dime, they called the cops. They ignored the signs you held up. It was no good going to the business district, Bad X always said. But G2 was drawn there like a fly to shit. One day that cheap bastard would hand him a buck and look him in the eye — straight in the eye. And when he did, he'd know and it would all be over. G2 to saw him here once. Maybe twice. It was always on a Wednesday, and that's when G2 went to the business district. When G2 was in town, he sat outside the Manhattan Club on Wednesdays and waited. The guy always had a buck in his pocket. He would come out of the restaurant, talking to some guy or gal like he didn't see anything else in the world. He'd reach in his pocket and drop the dollar in G2's cup. It was like an automatic response to the presence of the bum on the street, even though he never looked at G2 or acknowledged his existence. G2 often wondered if he treated any other bum the same way or if it was only him. G2 never told anyone else about it because nobody else came to the business district to panhandle and G2 didn't want them to. Sometimes another man in a suit would throw some coins in G2's cup. But it was always a single, wadded up dollar bill from this one. G2 wondered if he crumpled up the dollar so he could imagine he was throwing it away. Maybe he made a statement that said this was just a piece of trash and that old bum is a waste can. Or maybe it was an old unbreakable reflex to crumple it up. Was he angry at the dollar and that made him wad it up? Was he trying to make it small so it could be hidden and no one would see him give it away and say "that just encourages them?"

Gerald looked into a bum's eyes once — a long time ago. Really looked deep. At first, he didn't see anything but two eyes. They were a little glassy with the pupils dilated. Then Gerald began to read the silent desperation, the deep pleading in the bum's eyes. And Gerald knew he could help him. If he looked hard enough, G2 could see that expression in the eyes reflected back at him in the café window. But now he knew that he could not help, and the eyes retreated back into emptiness.

The man left the restaurant talking intently to his companion. G2 was sure the executive hadn't even seen him, but his hand snaked out of his pocket and a crumpled dollar bill fell into G2's cup. G2 watched until the man turned the corner and then he got up and ambled away toward the freight yard. Warm weather was coming. G2 reckoned he'd go spend some time up north.

♦♦♦

HE WAS RIDING the train across country to Disneyland. His parents had put the children to bed in the compartment next to theirs and went back to the lounge car to have a drink. There was never any alcohol in their home. His father didn't even allow beer or wine in the refrigerator. Knowing his parents were having a drink sent shivers down little Gerald's spine as he tried to go to sleep. Gerald had a vague memory of his father sitting at the kitchen table drinking a beer. He asked his father for a sip. It was a childish thing to do. Kids always want to try what their parents are doing, didn't they? But little Gerald's request shook his father. The man was at a loss for words. He looked at Gerald as though he'd never seen the boy before—had never contemplated the idea of being a father. In that long moment of eye contact, something unspoken passed between the two. Then, without saying a word in response, his father abruptly stood up and poured the beer down the kitchen sink. He opened the refrigerator, took out the remaining cans, popped the tops, and poured them out one by one. Turning to Gerald, his father said, "There is nothing to taste." There had never again been beer or alcohol in their house as far as Gerald knew. But when his parents went out alone, or—as now—escaped from the children to a lounge car, they returned smelling of the sweet perfume of wine. His parents were always happy when they returned from these dates, as if a great burden had been lifted from their shoulders for a while. When Gerald turned twenty-one, he had still never tasted a drop of alcohol. Somehow the train was inextricably linked to this memory. Feeling the rhythmic bump of the rails filled his mind with images of his parents coming back to their compartment, bouncing against the doors of the sleeper car as the train swayed on the tracks out of synch with the swaying walk of his parents. The sweet smell of wine or champagne on his mother's breath as she paused at their compartment to kiss the children in bed. The whispered good night to his little sister in the berth below him.

10

The thoughts were neither happy nor sad. They were simply part of the rails.

G2 wondered if his sister still lived in Seattle. It was a temperate climate in Seattle, but G2 still didn't like to spend the winter there. It was too dark. Even in the short hours of the day, the sky was dark with clouds. But his sister said she liked the area and that it was always green. She was 23 and newly married when G2 saw her last. That was a long time ago. He could tell she was embarrassed by him when she stepped outside her home to hug him and walk to a nearby coffee shop to talk. He didn't recall saying much, even then. He would get his act together, he had said. He just needed sometime to see the country. His clothes still fit him back then. And he'd managed to grab a disposable razor from an apartment complex garbage bin so he would look clean for her. But she could always see through him.

When Gerald was fifteen and Marian was eleven, he was left at home to babysit. He'd had a clever plan. As soon as she was asleep, he would slip out and meet his best friend Brian in the park. He tried to get her to bed and asleep as quickly as possible, but she resolutely refused to cooperate. "I don't want to be left alone," she said. "And if I go to sleep, you'll leave me alone."

Even in the coffee shop, she knew he wasn't coming back. She'd put a hand on the back of his and whispered, "Goodbye Jer-Jer." Then she left him in the coffee shop with both cups of coffee and five dollars as she hurried home. G2 recognized that gesture.

Gerald must have been about twelve or thirteen when his uncle died. His mother's brother fought lung cancer for three years before he succumbed. The mortician's makeup couldn't hide the emaciated remnant that lay in the coffin surrounded by flowers. Gerald and his sister followed their mother into the chapel and stood a respectful step behind as their mother stared at the corpse with tears silently streaming down her cheeks. Then she reached out and lightly touched her brother's hand and whispered, "Goodbye, Donny." She turned away, leaving Gerald and his little sister Marian staring into the casket. After only a moment, Marian mimicked her mother's gesture and said, "Goodbye, Uncle Don." Then she, too, turned to join her mother. Gerald hadn't wanted to touch the corpse but was overwhelmed by a morbid curiosity to find out what it felt like. He expected cold, but not quite as cold as it felt. Nor did Gerald expect the plasticene smoothness he felt. The flesh was completely flaccid. It was like touching a plastic wrapped piece of meat in the grocery store. It surprised Gerald so much that he forgot to say anything—just turned and went to sit with his mother and sister while a man who knew Don stood to talk about all the wonderful things he had done and what a good friend he had been. All through the funeral, Gerald kept rubbing his fingers together, still able to feel his uncle's dry, cold skin. When his father was killed in an automobile accident the next year, Gerald saw his mother and sister go through the same motions at the casket. Gerald declined to touch the man who had been his father.

G2 wondered if—in that coffee shop when his sister had said goodbye and touched him so many years ago—if his flesh had felt as cold and plastic to her as it did now to himself.

♦♦♦

G2 KNEW where the community center was; he'd been there before. It might be nothing—and if it was he was no worse off than before—but something deep inside told him this was the night. He wrinkled up his nose as he got closer, searching in the air for a tell-tale scent. He was almost to the door before he finally caught it. They were serving dinner for the homeless tonight. Dinners at community centers were always the best. You could go in and eat your fill of whatever they served, grab a few slices of bread to put in your bag, and leave without having to listen to more than a few God blesses, and maybe a prayer. There were always missions you could get a meal at, but the price of food was often to sit through a long sermon, sometimes even before they let you eat. They wouldn't let you bring wine into the mission and it was too late by the time you got out to get any. Some nights, Gerald was too hungry to resist. He didn't object to the sermons or what people believed and tried to get him to believe. He could even nod his head at what they said and whisper "God bless" back at them. But sitting sober at one of their sermons always started Gerald thinking. And thinking like that could make you crazy.

"Brothers and sisters," a preacher would start out and G2 would start asking himself if he was related to the preacher. And if he was related and everybody in the room was the preacher's brother or sister, then he must be related to everybody in the room — even the black men, the Asian whores, and the Mexican day-laborers. Now G2 knew none of them were raised in the same house he was. He was pretty sure his mother only had two children. But his father might have had children by as many women as he wanted. Of course he would have to travel all over the world to get Chinese and Mexican children. He'd be a regular George Washington who was father of his country. It just showed that religion started out lying in the first three words. Brothers and sisters. But they want people to believe really unbelievable stuff. G2 figured that if a preacher could make a bunch of bums in a mission believe they were his brothers and sisters, he was well on his way to making them believe any other thing he wanted to preach. G2 had long since learned how to talk like they wanted. Yes sir. I believe. Amen. God bless. If you tried to argue with them they couldn't let go. They'd talk you to death and you'd be lucky to get cold soup for dinner. But at community centers you just walked in on a night they were serving dinner and filled a plate with hot greasy pasta and ate. Nobody looked in your bag to see if you were carrying a bit of wine. Nobody preached more than a God bless. Nobody noticed when you stuck an apple and three slices of doughy Wonder Bread in your pocket and left. Nobody noticed you. They were good people.

That's the way it was with people. You get on in this world by nodding your head and keeping your eyes down. If you challenged people, they'd get you. G2 was never going back to Miami; that was sure enough. It was warm enough and you could sleep under the boardwalk or out on the beach without freezing to death as long as you weren't there during a hurricane and kept out of the way of the patrols. But G2 argued with a man in Miami. It was a long time ago, but people like that don't forget. It was nothing, really, but some folks just have to keep arguing even after you give up and move your bedroll to the other side of camp. Then they sneak up on you in the middle of the night and kick you in the gut with two of their friends, and you crawl away and slip into an empty boxcar on the first train heading north and you never go back.

♦♦♦

WHEN GERALD WAS A SENIOR in high school, he heard that his friend Jeff had been shot and was in a hospital in Milwaukee. Gerald was compelled to go visit the friend that he had played army with in the neighborhood. The Milwaukee County General Hospital was a bleak place. It was, Gerald found out, the same hospital that operated the TB sanitarium his father worked in during the Korean conflict and had a large wing that was considered a mental hospital. The medical facility was painted white throughout. Gray tile paved the hallways giving the impression of a stark black and white photograph of a hospital from another age. The people housed in its wards were mostly indigents who could not afford medical care. They were the people that Gerald's family had sometimes referred to as being "on the county." In the barbershop, Forrest the barber had once asked Gerald's father what ever happened to Old Man Sanders. He never came into the shop anymore. Gerald's father shook his head sadly and said, "Sanders lost his job and the bank took his house. He's on the county now. Probably can't afford a haircut." Jeff's ward had eight beds in it and Jeff was in the third on the right. As soon as he saw his one-time friend, Gerald couldn't for the life of him figure out why he'd come here. Jeff was stretched out on the bed flat on his back. The TV in the corner of the room was playing "The Edge of Night" and occasionally Jeff's eyes flicked toward it. The sound was turned so low Gerald could hardly hear it. Jeff's eyes watched Gerald come into the room but he didn't turn his head.

Gerald had dressed in his good slacks with a white shirt and tie on. He didn't know what the rules were for getting into a hospital. He'd just turned eighteen, but maybe they didn't allow people to visit who were younger than twenty-one. He'd chosen the tie carefully, opting for a straight narrow black tie instead of one of his father's broad multi-colored ties. Gerald's father had had a different tie for every day of the year. He wore a tie to the office every day. When he was killed, Gerald took all the ties into his own closet and a few white shirts as well. This was the first time he'd actually worn one of them.

"You some kind of a priest now?" Jeff asked as Gerald came up beside his bed.

14

"Naw. I just didn't know if they'd let me in to see you." Gerald could tell Jeff was in a sour mood, but who wouldn't be lying in this place flat on his back.

"Why'd you come? Nobody else came. None of the gang. Not one of the guys who said they were my friend. They all scattered and left me there."

"I don't know," Gerald said. "We used to be friends." There was a little silence with neither boy knowing what to say next. "What happened?" Jeff looked at him and managed to turn his head slightly to see him better.

"You with the cops?" Gerald shook his head. "They want to pin it all on me. I didn't do anything."

"What happened?" Gerald repeated.

"We decided to go down to Chicago and try to get some real booze. Guys had been drinking three-two all day and said we should have some whiskey. We all decided Chicago was the best place to go. We could get there where everybody looked the same, get some whiskey, and sit by the Lake and watch the sun come up. Then we'd roll back home. By the time we reached Milwaukee, everybody was tired of the whole idea. They said we might as well just get some booze in Milwaukee and light up the town. Norm was a Polack, so nobody'd be the wiser. We swung to the curb at the first liquor store we saw. That's when we realized nobody had any money to buy booze. So Norm, Kirby, and Sam said they'd go in. Billy was to keep the car running and I was to watch outside for the cops. Sam had a gun and they just walked in, waved it around and took a couple of bottles and money. I didn't know what was happening and I'd gone up to the corner to look for cops and was coming back when the three of them came running out of the store and piled in the car. Billy floored it with me running along behind to catch up. Bastard in the store came out with a rifle and plugged me in the back. Now I can't even piss by myself."

"Shit."

"Yeah. Shoulda just kept my head down and gone the other way." They were silent for a while. Gerald couldn't think of anything to say. He would never have been caught with those guys in the first place. He guessed maybe he was a goody two-shoes. But maybe that was why nothing bad ever happened to him. He just wasn't ever where the bad stuff happened.

"I ain't ever gonna get out of this hospital, am I?" Jeff asked. "You were the smart one Ger. You were always the smart one."

"I gotta go," Gerald said. "I'll come back and visit again."

"Yeah, you do that. Thanks for coming."

Gerald left and drove the two-and-a-half hours home lost in thought. Dad had been right. Just keep your nose clean and your head down and stay away from guns.

Jeff died later that winter.

♦♦♦

G2 HEARD SOMETHING he didn't recognize in the noise of the crowded street. The bumping throb hit him in the chest and made his lungs vibrate. It didn't seem to affect anyone else around, but it forced G2 to a wall for support. He must be crazy, thinking there was an earthquake when no one else could feel a thing. The teeth-shaking thump got louder and G2 could see a car—that was a Jeep, he remembered—approaching. As the Jeep went on past, the thumping gradually faded. That much echo in his chest made G2 feel empty. That must have been music, he thought.

There was a time when Gerald liked music. He was like any other teenager. He knew all the popular songs. They were good for getting to touch girls. Not all the songs. Some songs seemed to be made to keep people apart, dancing in their own little world as if no one else existed. One time Gerald took a girl to a dance and barely saw her all evening. When he took her home after the dance, she was effusive about how much she enjoyed herself, but she never went out with him again, even though they often went to the same dances and she never seemed to be with anyone else. There was some music, however, that seemed to make a girl melt into your arms—like at senior prom. It started out with everyone nervous about the big night, a corsage barely stuck with a trembling hand to the strap of a low-cut gown—that silent offer of a breast to caress, even if only with the back of one's hand. The music started with lively numbers and kids jumping around—dancing—frantically trying to burn off the sexual energy that had built with anticipation of the evening. Gradually, the mu-

16

sic slowed over the course of the night. Those who had outlasted the frenzy and were still on the dance floor moved together. By the end of the dance, their feet were barely moving, their bodies practically glued to each other.

Gerald drove his date home in his mother's old Ford Galaxy. She sat in the center of the front seat, snuggled under his arm, holding his right hand against her breast as he carefully maneuvered the big car down the country roads, never going faster than thirty. This was a moment he wanted to last. He remembered there was music then, too, on the radio. She used her free hand to tune to a late-night jazz station. When he pulled into her long farm-house driveway, he coasted to a stop near the barn and turned off the car and the lights, but left the radio on. She sank further into his embrace, giving him even more access to her breasts as she lifted her lips to kiss him. That first kiss after the prom was exquisite. He never wanted it to end. When it did, their hands had found every intimate part of each other's body and their breathing was shallow and intense. Gerald knew that this was the night and she was the girl. All he could think was a silent prayer that if they made love tonight he would never make love to another woman as long as he lived. She would be the one for him. But it wasn't to be. As if in answer to his prayer, she whispered to him, "Nothing that could last longer than tonight, Gerald. No long-term consequences, just the moment." They had cum together, but not through intercourse. When they were sated, she pulled her dress back together, kissed him one more luxurious time and got out of the car. Gerald jumped to walk her to the door, but she motioned him to stay. She walked to the back door of her house alone, turned to blow him a kiss, and then disappeared inside. They had only one date after that when she told him they were just too different to be dating. He was going to college and she was going to stay home and work. She just wasn't cut out to be a college guy's girlfriend. Later that year, she married a local farm boy and Gerald heard she had had two children by the time he finished college. Gerald had quit listening to music by that time. It was an interruption he didn't need. Even when he went to see a movie with his college girlfriend or watched television, he hated the way music manipulated his feelings. Music could trigger fear, tears, and lust. Nothing could be trusted to be what it appeared to be if there was music playing.

G2 moved his feet around to see if he could dance, but he couldn't remember any music. There was no rhythm, no sense to the movement of his feet, and no girl to hold. As he was intently trying unsuccessfully to remember a song — any song — from his teen years, a passerby dropped a coin in his cup, and all thought of music disappeared.

◆◆◆

G2 WAS LOOKING for an unoccupied corner in a retail area. People were more likely to give a handout in a retail area than in a business district. Business people were working and thought you should be, too. People who were shopping, though — especially those who bought things they didn't really need and felt guilty about — were in a spending mode and were sensitive to people who couldn't afford what they could. They could buy a quick indulgence for their greed and vanity with a few coins in his cup. You had to be careful of some businesses, though. He had once been taken by a well-meaning older woman into a beauty salon where she paid to have him barbered, shaved, and scrubbed. G2 came out looking young, clean, and smelling of some kind of fruit. He couldn't get a handout for a week after.

He turned a corner and walked into the trailing scent of a woman who had recently passed by. Even after such a long time, the scent had a familiarity to it, and a fragment of lyrics to an old song flitted through his mind. "Never gonna give you up — never gonna let you down." For a second he could feel the soft silkiness of Lori's hair against his face and the scent of her perfume filled his nostrils as he kissed her neck. A bus drove past and its exhaust erased the last lingering fragrance in the air.

He should have said goodbye.

He stood in place for a moment, bewildered by the sudden burst of memory that had come upon him. He was confused about where he was and blinked an unexplained tear from his eye. The world around him came crashing back in on his awareness. A crowd of people pressed toward him in the wake of a walk light. A gentle hand tapped him on the shoulder and G2 turned toward it quickly. "Sorry," said the young man who had touched him. "Didn't mean to startle you, but you'd better step back away from the curb. People are going to run you over out there. That bus mirror almost got you." G2 ducked his head and shuffled back toward the storefront on the other side of the walkway. To his surprise, the young man walked with him instead of turning to go away. G2 would normally not look twice at a boy this age. He'd learned long ago that males between 16 and 30 were simply too self-absorbed to notice a bum and give him a handout. This fellow looked like all the others. He wore khaki pants with a yellow polo shirt that had an animal stitched over his heart. Ear buds dangled around his neck and the cord led to his pants pocket. He wore loafers with pennies stuck in the tongue. This was not the kind of fellow who helped out bums.

"I'm gonna grab a cup of coffee," the guy said. "You want one?" Gerald barely nodded his head and the young man was off at a trot to a Starbucks on the corner. For a few moments Gerald considered leaving before the guy got back, but an elderly woman struggling past paused and fished in her purse, finally dropping two quarters in his cup. He bobbed his head toward her and quietly muttered "God bless," when the hand of another passerby reached out with a dollar for his cup. A small child, firmly gripped by his mother, smiled up at G2 and reached on tiptoe to drop a dime in G2's cup. The mother added a dollar. By the time the young man returned with coffee, there was $3.10 in his cup. "I hope you like cream. I just fixed it the same way I like mine. I'm Phillip, by the way. Oh, and here. They had these on sale in there because it's so late in the day." Phillip held out a plastic wrapped bagel sandwich. Gerald hesitated, though his mouth had begun to water. The sandwich had an egg on it. "Go ahead," Phillip encouraged him. "It's not like I paid a fortune for it or anything. They practically gave it away. Besides, I know where my next meal is coming from and I'll bet you don't. That's why I'm standing out here. My girlfriend is going to meet me. We're going shopping for an engagement ring and then out to dinner so I can propose properly. Did you ever get married, old man?" Phillip paused in his rambling only long enough to confirm that G2 shook his head. "Well, all that talk about how guys should buy a ring and surprise her with it is dumb. I mean, she's going to wear it every day for the rest of her life. She should have some say in what it looks like. And Lisa has some very strong opinions, let me tell you. You know those signs in a ballpark they put messages on? Some guys put their proposal up there and put the girl on the spot with 30,000 people watching. Man, if I did that I'd be a bachelor for life. No a eunuch. She'd make sure I was out of the running permanently. But you know what? If Lisa wasn't in my life, it would be empty. There just wouldn't be anything to give it meaning. Why would I want to be an engineer or move out west? I'd be pretty much like you. It's too bad you never found the right girl." Phillip kept talking, but G2 had stopped listening a long time ago. He was thinking again.

He should have said goodbye.

Everything had come so easy for him. He'd never really had to make a decision. Never in his life. He wore the same kind of clothes everyone else wore in school. He ate whatever his mother put on the table. He went to school and did what he was told to. "Keep your nose clean and your head down," his father always said. As a result, he got good grades. He scored high on his tests. He went to the first State University that accepted him. His schooling was paid for by scholarships. He met the perfect girl and they dated all through college. He assumed that someday she would simply tell him when they were going to get married and they would have a perfect life together. When he finally made a decision—the only decision he could remember ever making in his life—it all changed.

"You're drifting," Brian had said. "You honestly have the balls to complain that you never really had to work at anything. It all came too easy." Gerald and Brian had been friends for as long as he could remember and Gerald knew it had not all come easy for Brian. He'd worked hard in high school to get the grades Gerald got while playing ball. He'd taken loans to pay for college tuition that Gerald got on scholarship. Gerald not only respected Brian, he envied his ambition and drive. Brian knew what he wanted and wouldn't stop until he got it. Gerald had nothing more than a vague notion that he should do some good with his life. He had so much; it should help the world some way. But he didn't have an idea of what it should be. "What I'm saying is, don't throw it all away," Brian had said. "If you want to find meaning in life, then don't take the corporate job. Go volunteer. Do the one thing that no one else would do and make a difference."

It was two weeks before college graduation. Gerald finished his last paper and took his last exam, all the while wondering what would truly make a difference. If he could just change one person's life — change it for the better — then perhaps he could look at himself in the mirror and be proud of himself. Maybe he would know his life wasn't a waste — that it had meaning.

"Now there's a guy," Brian had said as they walked uptown after class, "who would give his left nut to be in your shoes." The man in question was dressed in fatigues. He stood in a light rain, staring out at traffic coming to a stop at the light. The sign he held in his hands read, "Homeless Vet. Need a little help. God bless."

"Hey man, wouldn't you like to be area sales manager for a hot new company?" Brian was never subtle in his approach. The homeless vet looked up and muttered "Fuck off" under his breath, but Brian was undeterred. "The only thing that separates you from this homeless guy is nobody dropped an opportunity in his lap. You want to do something good, for somebody, why don't you walk a mile in his moccasins and let him try on your wingtips. This guy would make something of his life if he had your opportunity, wouldn't you buddy?" Brian looked at the homeless vet and found him nodding his head.

The homeless man looked straight at Gerald and Gerald made up his mind on the spot. There was something in the man's eyes that had more spirit and fight aroused by Brian's pep talk than had ever found its way into Gerald. There was a kind of pleading in the man's eyes that captivated Gerald. For just a moment, Gerald could see the world through the other's eyes. It was harsh and grim. The man was building a wall between himself and the desperate gray world that surrounded him. The glimpse of hope when he looked at Gerald was a last chink in the wall.

Gerald's heart began to race as his breathing quickened. This could be possible. He could make a difference in the life of a man who desperately wanted what Gerald had. If Brian would agree to guide the man in his transition to a new, productive life, then Gerald could simply trade places — trade lives — with the homeless man. The way everything good just came to Gerald, he could earn his way out of homelessness in a year or two. Maybe he could develop a program based on his experiences — write a book. He'd do an analysis of life as a homeless man from the inside and he would be able to change not only this guy's life, but the lives of every desperate man and woman on the street. Gerald was young good things always came to him. It wouldn't be that hard and this guy would get the benefit of being Gerald for a year or two — enough time for him to be on-track for a good life of his own. It suddenly all made sense. Once he made his decision there was no reason to hold back or to wait. He had already earned his degree. Graduation was a mere formality. Within twenty-four hours, Gerald was homeless — G2, a man on the street — and the vet was dressed in Gerald's clothes, learning how to do Gerald's new job. Gerald didn't wait for graduation; didn't say goodbye. He walked out of his old life with the clothes on his back and disappeared.

Yes. He should have told Lori goodbye.

♦♦♦

THE SUDDEN DOWNPOUR had caught G2 unaware and he was soaked through. The weather had been getting warmer, but the rain was cold and G2 shivered. He wasn't supposed to get caught in bad weather. Homeless people, especially those few like G2 who eschewed shelters and semi-permanent encampments like tent city, were supposed to develop feral instincts that enabled them to get to shelter before bad weather hit. But G2 had been sitting near the river, hiding in a bend out of sight, while he nursed a magnum of wine. It had been a good day and he bought the largest bottle he could with his $7. He'd sat by the river all the previous night, sometimes sleeping while sitting up, then starting awake to take another little sip from the jug. In the morning there was still quite a lot of wine left in the bottle, so Gerald simply stayed where he was instead of panhandling at the freeway exit again. He'd spaced his little sips out all day long, so focused on his precious bottle that he didn't notice the clouds rolling in, or even the first few gentle spatters of rain until lightning split the night sky and the few drops turned to a downpour in seconds. When it started, G2 jumped up to run for cover, but a momentary disorientation as he bent to scoop up his bag and bottle left him unsure of which way to go. If he stepped out in the darkness the wrong direction he would fall into the river. It was some feet below the edge of the retaining wall and G2 knew that no matter how deep the water, he would be unable to climb back out. So G2 stood where he was, immobile as the rain washed over him.

"All things come to those who wait," his mother said to Gerald. It had been on the occasion of his 8th birthday and the bicycle from Sears that he had wanted for so many months sat next to the breakfast table. He hadn't dared to ask for it. His parents had a hard and fast rule to keep their children from being beggars. If you asked for it, you didn't get it. Gerald and his sister learned early never to ask their parents for so much as an ice cream cone when they were out. But they had also learned to express their admiration for things they desired. Whenever the family went to Sears, Gerald made a point of admiring the bicycle, sitting on it, and examining the price tag and information. His parents had noticed.

G2 still made a practice of never asking, even when he stood with his cardboard sign on a street corner. It said simply, "Thank you for your help. God Bless. G2" It wasn't clever, but it was the way G2 approached his life. Mad Jocko in Cincinnati was different. He boldly shook his sign at passersby. The sign read, "Ugly, broke, and homeless. Please help!" It worked all right for Mad Jocko. But he was crazy. Petey in D.C. usually sat outside the Greyhound Bus Station. He was pushy and the cops had been by to warn him off a few times. "Buddy, can you gimme a dime? Just a dime. I got ninety cents already and I just need one damn dime." He was pushy, but people listened to him. He got a lot of dimes and a lot of other change, too. He didn't hold any signs. He held a fistful of loose change that he was always looking at and counting. Then he'd look up suddenly as you passed by. "Hey Miss, could you spare a dime?" I got ninety cents already, but I just need another dime." Petey's favorite spot was next to the vending machines, but he never put money into them. Whenever someone got something from a machine, Petey would walk over when they left and check the change tray. Then he'd turn all of a sudden and catch a passerby. "Hey, you wouldn't have a spare dime would ya? I only got ninety cents here." Yeah, Petey did pretty good, but he was pushy.

G2 couldn't figure out which way to move as he stood soaking up the rain, so he tried to remember how much money he had in his pocket. He was sure he had more than ninety cents, but a dime really wouldn't do him any good. He started to shiver as the rain continued to pelt him. Each drop drove him closer to the ground until he was hunched into a little ball on the wet and muddy grass. One more sip from his precious bottle and G2 went to sleep with the rain still falling in torrents.

◆◆◆

IT WAS ONLY A FEW BLOCKS to the General's house. She was an old lady, retired from the Salvation Army. She had a modest house on the East Side, not far from the river. There, she lived an austere life, seldom straying from her living room. But it was known among a select few of the transients that she had half a dozen cots in her basement and no one in need of shelter for the night was turned away. G2 stood quietly at her door, waiting and dripping water on the steps. The door opened a crack and the General looked out. Then it was flung open wide.

"Heavens, man! You are soaked to the skin!" the General shouted. "Were you out in the rain all night?" G2 nodded his head. "Who are you? Is that G2?" G2 nodded again. "Haven't I told you to come any time you are in need? Come in here and let's get you dry and fed. Don't worry about the water; I have a mop." The General led G2 into the house and directly to the basement stairs. She grabbed a cloth shopping bag from a hook as they went. "There's only Bill O'Reilly down here at the moment and I guess he'll sleep another two hours. So here is a bag to put your valuables in. Empty all your pockets then throw your clothes out here on the floor." She turned the water on in a corner shower stall. It began to steam and G2's shivers shook him nearly off his feet. "Choose clothes out of the closet when you are done. I'll wash these and you can have them back if you want them. You use that yellow soap all over, even your hair, and use a razor, too. I want you clean and shaved when you sit at my table." The General left and G2 stripped and stepped into the steaming shower.

It took several minutes standing in the hot water before G2 stopped shaking enough to hold onto the bar of lye soap and scrub it on his body. It stung a little, but he knew it would kill the bugs that had infested his hair and skin. The General was fussy about cleanliness. G2's last suit of clothes had come from the General's closet. No doubt she would cut his hair off before nightfall. It would be cooler for the summer that way. Being clean and in clean clothes, the General would send him out to a job tomorrow. The General always had a job for you and you didn't have to stand in line for it. You just went to a mission or a legion hall or even a church. You swept and mopped all the floors and cleared the toilets. They gave you $20 and you left. It was good that you got that money, because you would be too clean and fresh-looking to make any money panhandling for a few days.

When he lived at home with his mother and sister, Gerald always had to be careful about how long a shower he took. If he used all the hot water his family would be upset, so his showers were hurried. By the age of fourteen he had become a speed masturbator. A few minutes in the shower with a bar of soap and Gerald could step out both clean and satisfied.

The General never seemed to run out of hot water, so unless there was a line of men waiting to get clean, there was no pressure to keep it short; but once he was warm, G2 felt no desire to stay in the shower as he had in his youth. G2 liked to be clean, but you couldn't really be clean and homeless. It wasn't that you couldn't clean up, but no one gave money if you looked too well cared for. He saw it all the time. The first week was hardest on people who had been cast from their former lives and had to find a way to make it on the street. Like Jane. Of course she didn't stay on the street too long—most women didn't. Women mostly went to the shelters and they got them into a program. Once you went into a program, you were expected to do what was necessary to get off the street. They got you a real job, a babysitter, and even dressed you for respectable work. But a lot of women didn't identify the shelters right away. They tried to make it on the street, sometimes living in their cars until the car ran out of gas and they couldn't move it again. Then it would get towed and from then on they'd never see it again No one who lived on the street could afford to get their car out of an impound lot. Jane had a car — and a baby. She ran away from an abusive boyfriend and suddenly discovered she had nowhere to go. She stood on a corner just off the exit ramp with a neatly lettered sign that said, "Homeless. Have baby. Need help." The "have baby" was a nice touch because children moved people to pity, but at the same time, if you didn't have the baby with you, they wondered if you really had a baby and if you did, who was watching it while you stood asking for a handout. And she didn't look homeless. She was young and pretty. Her hair was tied back in a ponytail. She was dressed in a white blouse and dark pants. And no one stopped to give her money. That first day G2 saw her, he was the only one who gave her anything. It took four days before the freshness wore off. She'd been parking in the Walmart parking lot each night and then using their facilities to clean her and her baby up in the morning. She parked the little car that she drove just across the street from where she stood with her sign. That fourth day, the baby was wailing in the car and she couldn't stand it. She wrapped the child up in a makeshift sling and carried her to the corner. Jane's hair came down out of its ponytail and her white blouse showed the dirt and wrinkles of three days wear. She couldn't get the baby to shush and before long tears were streaming down Jane's cheeks, too. It all seemed too much. But that day, Jane got $14 in gifts. It was enough to get food and cloth diapers for the baby. Jane was at that corner for two weeks before she found a shelter that could take her and her daughter in. The last time G2 saw her, her hair hadn't been washed in 10 days. Her clothes were rumpled because she slept in them as well as wearing them in the sun. The armpits were yellow and Jane cried almost constantly. But she got $15 - $20 each day standing at her freeway exit.

◆◆◆

"AND LOOK AT YOU, G2," the General said. "Once you are clean and shaved you are a young man, not an old one. Why I could send you to work tomorrow and you could be hired full time. No more sleeping on the streets. You'd just need to stay away from the bottle." Gerald was already feeling nervous about not having wine tonight before he slept. He was afraid he would start thinking again — thinking of what he had done and all that he had not done. If he went to sleep like that, he might think right through the night. Thinking like that could make you crazy. "I know you are not going to just quit drinking. G2. I've been there. A better Christian than I am would tell you that you just need to believe in Jesus and he will take away your thirst. But that sounds more like a threat to you than a blessing, doesn't it, G2? You don't want Jesus to take your thirst away. You are afraid of what might come instead." Gerald knew he would get a sermon from the General, but she didn't make you wait to eat while she preached. She sat at the table with you and scooped potatoes and boiled chicken onto her plate and preached with her mouth full. "People will tell you that life is too short to spend it at the bottom of a bottle, but they don't know, do they, G2? It's not too short, it's too long." The General took a long look at G2 and for a minute he thought she had finished the sermon before she finished eating. G2 scooped up a spoonful of peas covered with gravy, but almost didn't get them to his mouth when the General suddenly stood and left the room. G2 was her only guest at dinner tonight. He wasn't sure if it would offend her if he kept eating while she was gone. He sucked the spoon into his mouth and put it empty on his plate to wait. In a moment the General returned with a bottle and two glasses. "I haven't much," said the General, "but that which I have, I give you. In the name of Jesus, drink up." She poured out what wine there was left in the bottle evenly into the two glasses. She took one and pushed the other toward G2. "It's not much," she said, "but it should keep the ghosts away tonight." A tear welled up in G2's eye and he whispered, "God bless."

"I've seen you come through here once, twice a year for what now? Ten years? Fifteen?" the General mused aloud. "Those are the only words I hear you say. Well, it's okay if you prefer just to listen. If a man chooses just two words to say in his entire life, you chose good ones."

◆◆◆

GERALD WAS ELEVEN when the change started. It was a good year for most of his classmates. Most of the time, he could hide the thick bush of hair that grew in his groin. But his voice gave his early maturity away whenever he spoke. He spent a year excused from music class because he never knew what octave his voice would jump to when he sang. By the time he was twelve, that had been settled, but in spite of a sonorous bass voice that seemed out of place for his slight body, he couldn't carry a tune, let alone a harmony line. Classmates nicknamed him "Radio" because no matter what he said, it sounded like he was announcing it over the air waves. The voice had done as much as his grades in getting him into college and getting the sales job he'd been offered after graduation. He could make smooth, easy presentations and people hung on every nonsense syllable he uttered. He hated his voice for sounding like a trusted authority, even when he had no idea what he was talking about.

His voice made a liar of him and G2 had decided long ago that he would no longer lie. It was his first week in on the street and G2 discovered how little he knew about living there. But he'd always found his amicable approach to people and his mellow voice to open any door, so the first night he sought shelter under a bridge, he decided to ask a group of men where he could get a bedroll and some assistance. G2 was still clean-shaven and smelled of the last shower he took in his apartment before he locked the door and left. He'd stopped at MacDonald's for a double cheeseburger for a dollar, figuring he would make the twenty dollars he took with him when he left his apartment last. But his stomach was already complaining of too little to eat. He was still a few steps away from the men under the bridge when they stopped talking and directed their attention toward him. "Would you look at the college boy slumming," one of them said. "You here as a class assignment? You doing research?" said another. They were decidedly unfriendly, but G2 was determined to make friends in his new life.

"I am a little new at being on the streets. I was wondering if you could help me out. I don't even have a bedroll..."

"Where's your camera crew, asshole?" a black man asked as he stood and stepped toward G2. "You puttin' us all on TV?"

"No," G2 explained. "I'm not a reporter. I'm just newly homeless and I was hoping someone would show me the ropes."

"Ain't no ropes here. You live or you die. Right now you closer to dying."

"Sorry I bothered you," G2 said. All four of the men were now approaching him and his heart was racing. He thought there was a kind of brotherhood among the homeless. They took care of each other. He just wanted a little information.

"No cameras, huh?" said a dirty man with a long beard and no teeth. "No one to see you get kicked in the nuts?" It took only a moment before G2 realized the man was not speaking figuratively. He keeled over clutching his privates. "Nobody to see us check you for a microphone?" said the black man who had approached first. He dropped onto G2's stomach with his knee and ripped his shirt open to look for a wire. "Nobody to watch us check your pockets?" asked a man who looked like he was 80 and already had a hand in G2's pants pocket. "Look here what I found! He's got almost $20!" The fourth man, younger than the others, stood a few steps away and said nothing. G2 plead with him with his eyes, but the young man shrugged his shoulders and went back to the fire. "Twenty fucking dollars," said the old man. "Go home and have a bath and wash the stink of us filth off of you. I'd kill you for fifty dollars. Twenty dollars, I'll just kick you in the nuts again and tell you to get lost. And stay away from our bridge." G2 stumbled away from the men, beaten, dirty, and penniless. He slept the night in a doorway of a warehouse and prayed that he could get back into his apartment in the morning.

◆◆◆

"BRING YOUR DISHES TO THE KITCHEN," the General said. G2 looked nervously at his wine glass, still over half an inch in it. "Don't worry about the glass. You can take it downstairs with you." G2 breathed a sigh of relief and brought the rest of the dishes to the sink where he helped wash them. He had learned long ago to ration his wine, just a sip at a time. His last bottle had lasted him three days.

"I know what G2 means," the General continued in the kitchen. G2 looked at her curiously. He didn't make a secret of his name; he just never used it. "G2 means God's Grace. 'Twas by God's Grace you survived the night. God's Grace led you to my door this morning. Yes, God's Grace kept me alive to be here to help you. God's Grace will take us both to our final reward sooner or later. I don't threaten you with hell or damnation G2, for how could you tell that from what you suffer day by day. I don't threaten you because you live in a state of God's Grace." The General's voice turned to a sing-song adopted by many evangelists, G2 noted, but its hypnotic cadence drew him into her trance nonetheless. "Jesus was a transient with no possession but the clothes on his back, and so there is a special place for the homeless in God's Grace. Who else but the homeless, the downtrodden, the vagrant — who else but you, G2, could offer for the slightest kindness the two words that the world most needs — most desperately wants — to hear? God bless. You say those words and I am humbled for I hear in them God's Grace. God bless you, G2. Now take your cup to a cot downstairs and go sleep in peace."

The enthusiastic, if tuneless, voice of the General followed him down stairs. "'Twas grace that brought me safe thus far, and grace will lead me home."

◆◆◆

IT GOT TERRIBLY HOT in the summertime, even this far north. G2 considered going up all the way to the Canadian border to see if it would be cooler there. There weren't enough people further north, though. Perhaps it takes a village to raise a child, but it takes a city to feed a beggar. G2 had once tried to panhandle in the smaller towns but there simply weren't enough resources. G2 didn't mind moving from place to place, but with smaller towns and cities you had to move every few days. Some places were too small to stay a second day. In the city, moving meant a matter of blocks, not of miles. He could panhandle on Lake Street one day, Michigan Avenue the next, and at the expressway exit the next. He would never see the same person twice. People don't like to see panhandlers at the same place day after day, G2 had decided. It confirmed suspicions they were lazy and sparked fears they had moved in to stay. But as long as you didn't show up at the same place more than once a week, you were allowed to stay a few hours and then move on. Transient camps were another thing entirely. It seemed in the summer that wherever you gathered, the police were there in a day or two telling you to move on. G2 preferred to find a quiet spot to himself in the summer and although he moved frequently, he liked to stay near the lake.

◆◆◆

DURING SUMMERS BACK HOME, the family always went to the lake for at least two weeks, even after his father died. They would go "up north" with a dozen other families they knew and rent two room cottages on The Lake. Brian's family had never gone to The Lake for more than a day or perhaps a rare weekend. It was too expensive and Brian's father never seemed to have vacation time. But most summers Brian was allowed to come with Gerald for the whole two weeks. They weren't more than ten when they graduated from the flat-bottomed tippy-canoes to the motor fishing boat. "Tippy canoe and Tyler too," Gerald's dad would chant from the shore as the boys rolled the canoe over in the water again, scrambling over the sides back into it to paddle it half-submerged to the shore. But the fishing boat with its little four horsepower trolling motor meant the whole lake was theirs to explore. They started off one day to circle the lake, looking along the shore for a secret pirate's cove. It took them an hour to row the boat back across the lake from the far side when they ran out of gas in the little boat. No one actually used the fishing boat for fishing. The adults spent their time watching the children play — or sometimes waterskiing. They ate hamburgers or hot dogs from the grill for dinner every night and the children were left in the care of inattentive teenagers on Friday and Saturday nights when the adults went into the supper club in town. No matter what they got up to while their folks were gone, the kids were sure to all be in bed when the parents returned after midnight. After Gerald's father died, Brian's mother would sometimes join them for a week. She would sit with Gerald's mother at the table or on the porch swing talking in hushed tones. Most nights half a dozen adults would gather at one or another's kitchen table to play pinochle. When it was finally dark and the children were sent to bed, they could hear the low voices and laughter as the grown-ups played their games. After Gerald's father died, however, his mother stopped playing cards. She didn't have the energy to stay up that late any more, she said. When they turned 16, both Brian and Gerald declared that they didn't want to go to any stupid lake that summer. Gerald's mother seemed to breathe a sigh of relief at that news and cancelled the cabin reservation. They never returned to the lake as a family.

G2 returned every summer in his mind as he slept beneath a park bench near the water.

◆◆◆

THERE WEREN'T MANY FAT PEOPLE among the homeless, and morbid obesity was almost unknown among those who had been homeless for a few years. William McKinley Smith III was a noted exception. Well over six feet tall, Mack as other transients called him, was also over 300 pounds. It was an accidental encounter that put G2 in Mack's company headed for the local food shelf. Accidental in that Mack had fallen over G2 in the park late the night before. Mack had narrowly avoided crushing G2, having landed on his legs and not his torso. G2 thought that perhaps he should not have curled up in his bedroll so near the dumpsters, but there had been a soft bit of unmown grass here next to the trees. The trees masked the dumpsters from view in the park and thus hid G2 as well. It seemed ideal at the time, but the next morning being garbage pick-up, Mack was making the rounds to collect whatever he could find to eat. He had stumbled on a box with three stale donuts in it and was retreating from the dumpster when he stumbled over G2. He gobbled down his treasure and then lay down next to where G2 was and went to sleep. G2 considered moving elsewhere, but his spot of grass was still soft and Mack's bulk blocked the chill breeze that was blowing off the lake. G2 fell back to sleep, comfortable in the knowledge that Mack would not ask to share his wine. Food was to Mack what wine was to G2. He loved eating and couldn't care less what it was he ate. He didn't love food; he loved eating. When he had eaten enough, he slept. Stories G2 had heard said Mack had money. Lots of money. But Mack chose to live on the streets and eat rather than living in a house and going hungry.

"You know the problem with this world?" Mack asked G2 as they lumbered toward the food shelf in the morning. "There're too many fat people. Look at them. Mamas, babies, grandpas. All eating too much food instead of sharing with those in need." It was obvious to G2 that Mack considered himself in the latter category and not the former. "The men in my family have always been big. My grandpa, William McKinley Smith Senior, had a special chair built at the head of the family table, just to hold him. It was a good chair. I sold it for $400 in 1985. The man who bought it was small by comparison to my grandpap. My father, William McKinley Smith Junior was said to have eaten a whole ham at one sitting — breakfast, no less. Now there was a man who loved his food as much as he loved his wife. We joked that if he ran out of food, she would be his next dinner. I'm as big a man as they were. It takes food to keep a body like mine going. If I ever have a son, he will be William McKinley Smith the Fourth and he will be a big man, too."

Brian's father was the biggest man Gerald had known when he was growing up. Howard was six feet five inches tall and dwarfed everyone else that Gerald knew. Once they had attended a Fourth of July parade together. Brian and Gerald must have been eight or ten, he thought. They were caught in the back of the crowd and Howard had lifted one boy up on each of his shoulders. There they sat through the entire parade, able to see every float and marching band and clown throwing candy. They felt like giants. Howard worked in an automobile factory and Gerald thought he must be so strong from having to build cars all day. He hoped that one day he would be big and strong enough to work in a factory like Howard. It seemed so much better than wearing a tie and sitting in an office all day like his father did. But Gerald had grown up slightly built, while Brian towered over him. Genetics were at work. Neither Brian nor Howard was fat, though.

"My mother, God bless her, used to say Dad and me would eat her out of house and home. I guess she was right," Mack continued between great puffs of breath. "She's been gone — oh — 15 years now, I suppose. She left me the house in her will. But when I had to choose between food and shelter, I sold it. Just can't see wasting money on things like insurance and electricity. "You can't eat taxes," my Dad used to say. When the doctors told him he had cancer and chemotherapy killed his appetite, he figured he'd rather die fast and save Mom the burden of wasting money on his healthcare. Wrestling his body out of the car in the garage took the entire fire department when he killed himself. But taxes paid for that service, at least. If there ever comes a time when I can't feed myself, I'll end it quickly, too. But in the meantime, there's the food shelf. I'll just thank you now for coming here with me, G2, in case I forget later."

They entered the facility and took their places in line. It was too crowded for G2 under normal circumstances, but Mack's constant talk kept him focused. Mack told him which items to pick, avoiding things that had to be refrigerated or cooked. Gerald would never have chosen things in cans because they were heavy and he didn't have a can opener. But Mack insisted that he take as many cans of beans and of soup as they would allow. Three cans of Spam and a surprisingly heavy bag of carrots topped off their allotment. They carried their bags out of the food shelf and into the bushes where Mack had carefully stowed his grocery cart the night before.

That was something G2 did not understand. He had been given a cart once. It was very nice. A group of well-meaning folks started handing out grocery carts to the homeless. The carts had been modified so they folded out into tents. You had shelter anyplace you went and a place for your possessions in the cart. "Everyone should have a roof over their heads," the happy social workers said as they shoved carts into the hands of the homeless. G2 kept losing track of his cart. He didn't have anything to put in it and it seemed senseless to push around an empty cart to sleep under at night. When the weather got bad enough to need that kind of thing, G2 moved further south. One day he hopped a train and left the cart tent sitting beside the switch yard. He supposed someone had found it and taken it. He certainly wasn't going back to Oakland just to find out.

"Now, G2," Mack was saying, "you take these." He handed G2 six huge carrots. "Nothing like a couple bites of carrot if you get to feeling hungry. Six carrots — why that might last a man like you the rest of the summer. And don't think I forgot something. We'll just walk over to Copeland's now and get you yours. Push this cart for me till we get to the sidewalk there." Mack was already scooping beans out of an open can into his mouth. G2 kept wheeling the cart while Mack ate, all the way to the liquor store. In return for his services at the food shelf, G2 parted company with Mack having six fat carrots and a fresh box of wine. It was worth having been almost crushed in the middle of the night.

◆◆◆

NIGHTTIME WAS ALWAYS THE WORST. That's when G2 felt the feeling that wasn't there the most. There was supposed to be a feeling of deep joy or contentment or satisfaction or peace that made everything else okay. That was the way it was supposed to be when you did something good for someone — when you sacrificed yourself for a cause. But when everything was quiet and G2 had taken his last sip of wine, his brain went haywire and he kept thinking. He kept seeing things the way he'd seen them as a child.

Like the time his father took him fishing in the river. Dad always said he liked to fish. It was a real pain in the ass for Gerald, and somehow he got the impression that no matter what his father said, fishing was something he'd once done to have food, not because he enjoyed it, and he wouldn't be doing it now if he didn't think it was the right thing for him to teach his son. "Give a man a fish and he'll eat for a day," his father said. "Teach a man to fish and he'll never be home for supper." Then he'd laugh a kind of hollow laugh that was supposed to mean they were sharing quality leisure time together when they both wanted to watch football on TV.

Gerald experimented with several methods of putting a long red night crawler on the hook. There was the one jab and throw it in the water method. Just stick the hook through the fattest part of the worm and drop your line in the river. The bobber would jump once in the water and Gerald would pull his line out, the hook empty. His father called that "feeding the fish." "Too easy for the fish to eat and run," his dad would say. So Gerald tried his father's method — the accordion technique. You stuck the hook through the worm, then folded it over and stuck it again and again. This meant that no part of the worm was far from the business end of the hook. In Gerald's experience it just meant the bobber went down two or three times before he pulled up an empty hook. "Clever fish," his dad would say, pulling up his own empty hook. Gerald couldn't remember if he'd ever actually seen his father catch a fish. He asked his dad if all this hooking a worm didn't hurt them. "No," his father said, "they don't feel anything. Worms are natural fish food. That's what they were made for." That's when Gerald came up with the thread the pipe method. He started at one end of the worm and threaded the hook up the length inside the worm. There was still enough worm left off the hook to wiggle good, but no fish was going to eat him off the hook. Gerald's next big lesson was taking the hook out of a fish. With the worm still thrashing around in the fish's mouth and the fish flopping around on the shore trying to figure out what it was doing out of the water and why it couldn't get the worm the rest of the way down its throat, the slippery fish was almost impossible to hold onto. When Gerald finally got the hook out, the fish flopped back into the water before he could get the stringer through its gills. His dad said, "It was too small to eat anyway." They packed up their fishing gear and left the river. On the way home, they stopped at the schoolhouse where the boosters club was holding a fish fry. His dad bought two tickets and they went in. "Give a man a buck and you'll have all the fish you can eat," his dad laughed. Gerald and his dad then proceeded to see who could eat the most pieces of fish, all the time making jokes about which one was the one that got away. "Take that you worm-thief," his dad said while dunking a deep-fried perch in a big bowl of tartar sauce.

G2 still wondered if it was true the worms didn't feel anything. They sure squirmed around a lot. He'd tried fishing once or twice when he couldn't seem to find a hand-out anyplace, but the big carp he caught never seemed to cook all the way through and tasted muddy when he finally got a mouthful of the mostly raw fish in his mouth. It didn't seem like the worm had all that much time to think about what it was feeling, though. They were born to be fish food. They got picked up, stuck on a hook and eaten. It took longer to kill, clean, cook, and eat the fish. The worm should have felt something in those final moments, though. Pride that it was being sacrificed for the greater good of humanity or something. Anticipation in knowing someday the executioner would be dead and the worms would crawl in and out like that grade school verse said. "When you see a hearse go rolling by, you wonder who is the next to die. The worms crawl in. The worms crawl out. The worms play pinochle on your snout." G2 was sure the worms were crawling in and out of his father now, if there was anything left to crawl through. He wondered if his mother was still alive. It had been about thirty years since his dad died. What was still left? G2 tried to remember what the casket had looked like. No worm would ever be able to get through that concrete vault and industrial steel, hermetically sealed casket they'd put him in. How was the body supposed to return to dust wrapped up like that? G2 certainly didn't want to be sealed up in some aluminum and concrete Tupperware. When Brian's grandmother died, they burned her up. Nothing left but ashes and G2 was pretty sure the worms didn't eat ashes. Maybe if G2 was lucky, he'd drop off a cliff somewhere and they'd never find his body. Then the worms could all be happy for a moment of triumph before another smart ass kid threaded it on a hook and fed it to the fish.

◆◆◆

GRANNY SAL was in her usual position outside Walgreen's Drug Store. If she hadn't been there, people would be concerned. As far as G2 knew, she had been there every morning for years. She sold the local street paper for a dollar and always seemed to have a stack of them beside her little campstool. The publisher sold the papers to Sal for thirty-five cents, so G2 figured she made a pretty good profit and could buy food and wine anytime. She lived in a shelter where she paid $5 a night for a cot, a meal, and hot water. G2 figured she had to sell ten newspapers every day to pay for her sojourn. That was a lot of work for very little benefit, but it had made Granny Sal a fixture at Walgreen's. Everyone knew her, and she knew a little something about everyone.

When G2 was new to the streets, he thought he would get a job writing for the street papers. Some of them paid fifty cents a column inch for stories, but a column inch was a lot of words, especially when the two-page story he wrote had been cut by an editor to a two-inch blurb. G2 decided right then that he would save all the words he was writing and get his book published someday and then he would be set for the rest of his life and wouldn't have to panhandle anymore. The longer he wrote, the less he could remember what he was writing about. Things kept distracting him. For example, there was the blue Volvo, license number 123REJ that was always parked at the free clinic. Now 123REJ was a very interesting license number. If G2 was inventing license numbers, that was one he would have invented. 123 REJect. It was easy to remember. "Elegant," he remembered a college composition professor saying about his writing once. G2 could think of a lot of elegant license plate numbers that started 123. 123GO. 123ABC. 123HIC. People might have trouble with that one, he thought. Who would know that it meant "Here I Come?" He'd have to work on that one. He had jotted it down on a piece of paper and carefully folded it up in his pocket with the little stub of pencil that he had. Sometimes he saw one of his license plate ideas on a car. SPY007. That was his. He must have lost that piece of paper and someone from the license bureau found it and made the plate. Or probably it was those punks.

G2 had been in a rough part of town, looking for a place to sleep for the night that wouldn't be raided by the police. They were making sweeps through some of the best places to sleep and forcing people to move away. The bridge under which he'd spent nearly a week out of the rain had been cleared the day before. He was walking down a street just after dusk, looking for an out-of-the-way place to lie down and have a sip of wine when he was distracted by a license plate that said "PMPRD." It was a shiny car and looked out of place on the dirty street. He stopped and fished out his pencil and a slip of paper. While he was concentrating on the license plate, trying to puzzle out what it meant, he had missed the approach of three men until one grabbed him by the collar and hauled him back against a brick wall. "Wha dya thing ya doin. Ya innersted in Big Jim's wheels?" "You under cover? A cop?" "Just a wino, bro. Dummy." The words came too rapidly for G2 to sort them out, but when he tried to protect his bag, it earned him a punch in the stomach. The canvas bag was ripped off his shoulder and the contents dumped out on the ground. One of the men grabbed the paper bag with his wine in it. And unscrewed the cap. He poured back a slug of the precious liquid and then spewed it out of his mouth all over G2. "Tha' shit's nasty," he said, and flung the bottle against the wall where it shattered. G2 wept more for the bottle than from the punch. "My bitch tasted like that, I'd make the dog lick her." "Look at this: A journey alone by G2. Dude's a god-dam writer. Les see what you wrote." G2 always intended to write the story of being homeless and sell it. Now these punk bastards had it. He screeched as he launched himself toward the punk with his words and was rewarded with a fist to the jaw that sent him back into the wall. He hit his head on the bricks hard enough to stun him and he slumped to the sidewalk. "Nothin' here but license numbers," the punk laughed. He didn't know which one. Papers were being scattered. Ten precious pieces of paper and his pencil. All the work since he'd been homeless. G2 raised a hand just to have it slapped down. "You stay 'way from the Pimp Ride, asshole. We fine you here again, you a dead bum." Someone kicked him and the three started laughing as they walked away looking at his sheets of paper. "Big Jim's waitin'," he heard them say.

Those punks probably went to jail with his license numbers. That's where they made license plates – in jail. They went there with his numbers and made them into license plates and that's why now G2 saw license plates that he wrote on cars that were on the street. He was keeping track of which ones were his ideas. It was a long time ago, but G2 remembered.

♦♦♦

GRANNY SAL RECOGNIZED G2. Granny Sal recognized everyone. She greeted her customers by name, even the ones in suits and shiny shoes. A lady came out of the drug store with a cup of coffee. "Granny, I got you a cup of coffee and a donut. Here's a dollar for the paper." Granny Sal smiled her gap-toothed grin and took the money and food, handing the woman her paper. "And how's that little Josh?" Granny asked. "He over his cold now?" "He's doing fine now, Granny," the woman said. "He'll be back in school Monday." "That's good," Granny Sal said. "I got a little something for that cute little boy." She dug in her apron pocket and produced a wrapped piece of peppermint candy. "This'll help his little sore throat. You give it to him and tell him Granny Sal says to get well soon." "Thank you Granny." The woman took the newspaper and the peppermint and headed for her big SUV in the parking lot.

Granny Sal sat on her little camp stool with her legs stuck straight out in front of her. Anyone coming up that side of the street had to either step over her, or step off the curb to go around her. But no one seemed to mind. Granny Sal had a little something for everyone and everyone, it seemed had something for Granny. She saw G2 as he approached and struggled up off her stool to stand. She was scarcely taller when she stood up than she was when she was sitting on the little stool.

"G2! You're back," she said, holding out her arms to hug the man. G2 quietly came into her arms, waited patiently while she hugged him and watched her sit back down on her camp stool. "You've been gone a long time, G2. You just passing through?" He nodded and looked up at the sky. "Yes," Granny said, "almost time for the weather to change. You'll be heading south with the birds, I suppose. What's it like in the South? I imagine it's all sunny beaches that you vacation on in the winter, isn't it G2? Pretty girls in bikinis bringing you wine with a little umbrella in it. How I envy you traveling around. I can't move from my spot, I tell you. Wouldn't last a day if I had to find a new place to sleep every night. And my customers — what would they do? If I wasn't here for them, they'd be in an awful fix. I figure this stool is where I live my life and this stool is where I'll die one day." G2 liked Granny Sal. She never expected him to say anything. She made up all the stories about him that she told and he believed her. Yes, he would head south for the winter and sit on fine sunny beaches in Florida. Maybe he would just go all the way out the end of Key West and then dive right into the ocean and swim to Cuba. He could get on a cruise ship as a porter and go on down to Rio in South America. All he had to do was listen to Granny Sal.

"I have something for you, G2," she said. "Been saving it because I knew you'd come back." She searched pockets that seemed to be hidden all over her clothes. G2 reckoned that if you emptied out all her pockets, she'd be skinnier than his arm. Finally she pulled out a tiny pad of paper and a pencil that was three inches long. It didn't have an eraser. "Here we are," she said. "I just found this little notebook. Some of the pages are used, but there's lots of new paper in there. And this pencil? Would you believe they were giving them away at a street fair? See, it says WXRX on the side of it. A radio station that was playing music so loud it hurt my ears a block away. But they had pencils they said were for golfers. As soon as I saw it, I thought G2 don't play golf, but he still needs a pencil. This will help G2 write his novel, I said to myself. Maybe he'll publish some articles in *The Roof* and my customers, right here on this block, will read what he wrote in this little notebook. You'll be a great writer someday, G2. And I want an autographed copy of whatever it is you publish. Don't forget your Granny Sal."

G2 took the offered pencil and paper. It wasn't every day that he got new paper, and the pencil he had been using earlier in the day was only as long as the first joint on his thumb. It still had some lead, though. G2 would whittle it down with a piece of broken glass and still get a page or two out of it.

Gerald played golf once in college. He figured that there wasn't much to it. You swung a club at the ball and then putted it in the hole. That much, at least, was just like playing miniature golf. Easier, since there were no windmills. The recruiter that was interviewing Brian and Gerald in college took them to Lake Geneva and treated them to a weekend at the Playboy Club. This was the high life he was telling them they would enjoy as sales managers. There were half a dozen other recruits, three Regional Sales Managers, and the National Sales Manager. Golfing was a requirement. Gerald and Brian rented clubs and decided to share a single set. The $40 greens fee included a golf cart and the friends were joined by Steve, the National Sales Manager and a recruit from Chicago named Ed. Ed was a serious golfer. Every drive went straight down the fairway. He was shooting just over par at the seventh hole. Steve was a serious golfer, too, but didn't have any of the skills that Ed had. He replaced several balls that went into the rough or water hazards and it seemed that every stroke was accompanied by a string of curses. After three straight balls went into the water off the sixth tee, Steve turned to the others and in a burst of frustration said, "Well boys, now you know the National Sales Manager really sucks cock." There was a long pause before he continued in a somewhat lower voice, "I'd appreciate it if you didn't tell that to the other managers." Brian and Gerald nodded seriously while Ed guffawed. Apparently it had been a joke. Gerald's play was also frustrating, though he wasn't as prone to fits of tantrum like Steve was. It just didn't seem that he could get the ball in the air. He hit line drives that barely cleared the ground and at one point simply used his putter to hit the ball seven times down the fairway to the green. At the ninth hole, a short one, Ed handed Gerald a driver from his bag and said "Here. Try this and keep your head down and your eye on the ball." Gerald followed the instructions and swung hard at the ball. He connected. The ball soared high into the air. It overshot the par 3 hole by fifty yards, and they heard it hit pavement near the trees. The private airstrip was just on the other side of those trees and all four men watched as the ball took a long high bounce and came down on one of the single engine planes parked near the runway. They looked in shocked amazement as Ed took the driver from Gerald and put it in his bag. "I say we call that a hole-in-one for everyone on the team," Steve said. The four men moved quickly to the tenth tee where three bunnies were serving beers.

◆◆◆

G2 LOOKED AROUND for something to write in his new notebook while Granny Sal watched. There were cars stopped for the traffic light at the corner. A man pushed a shopping cart out of the drug store and over to his Toyota in the parking lot. G2 couldn't figure out how a person could buy so much in Walgreen's. A young couple sat at the bus stop, cuddled together, occasionally turning to kiss each other as they talked quietly. Two crows noisily fought over a MacDonald's bag in the parking lot and beyond them a cat stalked forward planning a stealth attack. An airplane streaked overhead leaving a contrail, but just too far away to be heard above the din of the city traffic. When G2 opened his eyes wide and really looked at the world around him, there was so much that he was almost overwhelmed. Then he saw it and all his attention narrowed to a single point. The noise and distractions of the city fell away, leaving him with a moment of crystal clarity as he opened his notebook and wrote: CC1492.

◆◆◆

G2 AWOKE in the middle of the night. The effect of the wine was wearing off. The blank in his head was already being replaced by thoughts, but that wasn't what woke him. There was a tension in the air. G2 knew he wasn't the only one huddled beneath his thin blanket awake. It could be police, but it was too quiet. Gangs staking out new turf? Or...

G2 gripped his canvas bag in one hand and a corner of his blanket with the other in case it turned nasty and he had to flee. But it might be otherwise. He even dared to hope it was. He saw lights flicker across the camp. One stopped near Big John. G2 could see Big John's wide open eyes as the flashlight hesitated on them and then moved down. A shadow stepped between G2 and the light and Big John was lost.

"Here's a nasty looking bum," a young man's voice said as a light shone in G2's eyes. "Doesn't smell too bad either. You're lucky."

"Oh god. Do I have to?" a young woman spoke from behind the light.

"Nope. Don't have to. I'm just here to protect you and verify the kill. I don't care whether you do it or not," the man said.

"Let me see," she said. The man reached down and flipped the thin blanket off G2. G2 kept his grip on the corner so he wouldn't risk losing it altogether. The flashlight beam moved down his body.

"Oh my god! He's got a boner already," she exclaimed a little too loudly. Her body guard hushed her.

"We don't make noise; we don't draw a crowd," he said. "Now are you in or out?" She giggled.

"Just a handjob, right?"

"That's all," he said.

"Let's do it," she whispered hoarsely. The man—G2 could tell he was just old enough to be called a man, maybe twenty years old—leaned down and whispered in G2's face.

"This nasty little slut wants to touch your boner, old man," the boy said. "You okay with that?" G2 nodded slightly. "The rule is she touches. You don't. Understand?" G2 nodded again. The boy pointed his flashlight down at G2's hard-on. "He's all yours, Lindsey," he said.

The young woman knelt beside G2's thigh. She was just close enough that G2 could make out a few details of her face and figure. She was dressed like a hooker in a short skirt and halter top. She had make-up painted on in mad swirls. It would be impossible to recognize her if she washed her face. He glanced up at the boy who had his cell phone out pointing the camera at her. Tentatively she reached out and touched the tent in G2's trousers. He caught his breath.

Sex wasn't unknown among the homeless. G2 knew almost as many lost women as men, but they often stayed apart. It seemed the women sought out the shelters if they weren't attached to a man. It was safer. But attachments did happen—sometimes for only a night, sometimes for a year or more. G2 had never been able to make it last more than a week or two. There was that one—Susan, that was her name—that stuck close to G2 for nearly a month. They had early morning sex under their blanket half a dozen times. It was comforting. It was always quiet, like a secret shared in the darkness when you didn't want to attract attention. People got ideas if they saw you copulating. G2 wasn't strong enough to fight off another man. It started with them sharing a bottle of wine. Most things started that way. They made that bottle last, having just a sip at a time for hours. Susan knew how to make wine last—just little sips and no long gulps. She treasured it as much as G2 and they left a sip in the bottle for morning. It was too late to make it to a shelter, so Susan just lay down next to him and went to sleep. He woke up in the middle of the night with a raging hard-on and couldn't figure out why. Susan hadn't seemed to mind that he was poking out at her and had been accommodating. Usually, they slept back to back, sharing a warmth and protection. Sometimes one would roll into the other and if the camp was still dark and quiet, they'd find their way together. One night, Susan didn't join him at his fire. The weather was getting cold and the next morning G2 hopped a southbound freight train. He always wondered what happened to Susan and if they would meet again. She sometimes laughed and it was good to hear.

But Susan wasn't a midnight angel like the one stroking his cock now. Gerald didn't dare move for fear the angel would dissolve into mist. Everyone had a different theory about midnight angels. Some said they were prostitutes doing charity work. Some said it was college girls who had to do it to get into a sorority. Skinny Eric the Twig had a sign that said "Will knock you up for cash." He'd once been paid to get an anonymous girl pregnant. There were those who held that the midnight angels didn't exist at all and said men made them up out of their dreams. Bald Sam bragged that they visited him three or four times a week and everyone knew he was a liar. G2 wasn't sure what to believe, but he wasn't about to move for fear it would stop.

"I thought you said it would only take a minute," the girl said. "He's got the stamina of a horse."

"He just wants to see your titties, nasty girl," said the boy. "Probably hasn't seen titties in ten years. Go ahead and show him what a nasty slut you are." She reached up with one hand and untied her halter top. G2 watched as the pale white globes came into view. He tried to memorize every detail. How big her breasts were; which direction her nipples pointed; how her neck touched her shoulder. It was all too much to take in. G2 closed his eyes and exhaled.

"O, yuck! Look at it all; it's all over everything," she exclaimed quietly. "God, it's on me."

"Here's a towel. Clean up and let's go," said the boy. G2 didn't move — didn't open his eyes.

"Is he dead?" he heard her say.

"Who knows? Let's get out of here." She dropped the towel, damp with his cum, on top of G2. He heard their steps fade away as he rolled over under his blanket and slept.

◆◆◆

G2 WAS SICK. Really sick, he knew. It wasn't just DTs, even though he hadn't had a drink in three days. He wasn't even sure he wanted a drink. The thought of wine hurt his stomach. He was hot and his clothes were soaked through with sweat. His head hurt. His skin hurt. His heart was in his throat. And his throat hurt. G2 needed to get to the clinic. They'd give him something at the clinic and he would be okay.

Gerald had been sick when he was eight years old. It was a terrible time. His father had taken him to the YMCA the previous year for swimming lessons and when they found Brian and his father and the father/son combinations of three other nearby families, the dads decided to start a local club of Indian Guides. Once each month the boys and dads would get together at one of their homes and do crafts, listen to stories, and eat treats. Monte's dad had shown them all how to make a crystal radio. It was almost magical and was the first radio of his own that Gerald had. It had no speakers, but a single tiny ear bud that stuck in one ear. When they finished the project, Monte's Dad wrote a note attached to each crystal radio: "Ground me, Dad!" Gerald's father took him to the laundry room in their home and attached the wire with an alligator clip to the valve on the washing machine's cold water line. Gerald put the ear bud in his ear and carefully turned the tuner until a crisp voice broke through the crackling static. It was a miracle. Gerald could tune in three stations on his crystal radio. He listened to the news, some gospel music — interrupted by Edwin Everest who preached at a big church downtown and gave sermons on the radio every night — and Fred Newman's Dinner Hour. Fred made random phone calls at 6:00. If your phone rang at 6:00 you had to answer "Dinner Time!" If you said "Hello," Fred would say "You said Hello and your chance is go." You knew then that you missed the dinner basket that Fred delivered to the winners. Gerald listened to Fred at 6:00 every night on his crystal radio, sitting cross-legged on top of the dryer in the laundry room, listening with the other ear for his phone to ring.

Then came the Indian Guide campout. For weeks the boys and dads worked at Mark's house to cut long birch poles to the same length, lash the ends together, and set them up. Then the dads would spread the big brown canvas tarp over the frame and everyone would crawl inside. There was scarcely enough room in the tepee for the ten of them and the dads joked about having to sleep in layers. All summer the boys practiced putting up the tepee and building campfires at Mark's house, under the careful supervision of their dads. The big campout was to be on Saturday. Their tribe would join all the others sponsored by the local Y at a state park 50 miles away. Dennis's father had a pickup truck and on Friday they loaded it with the poles and everyone's packs so they could leave Saturday morning. Everyone went home in a frisson of excitement to sleep in their beds one more time before the campout. Gerald could hardly get to sleep.

At midnight he woke up. He had to go to the bathroom. He was shaking and cold, but his sheets and pajamas were soaked through with sweat. Once he sat on the toilet, he didn't want to get up and tears started running down his cheeks. His mother was the first to get up to see what was wrong, but his father was beside her as soon as she called. "He's got a fever," she said. His dad asked him questions about what hurt and Gerald croaked out "I'm just nervous about the campout." His voice didn't sound right. And it hurt. "You're a little young to have nerves like this," his father said, smiling at him. "I'm afraid you don't have to worry about the campout. It looks like you'll be spending the day in bed." Gerald was devastated. Nothing was more important than the campout with his friends, the Indian Guides in the State Park fifty miles away from home. The tears wouldn't stop coming down and every hot drop stung his cheeks. His mother tried to get him to take an aspirin, but he couldn't swallow it until she crushed one up in a teaspoon of water and he drank the bitter pill. In the morning, Gerald woke with the pain searing his throat and could hear his mother and father talking about a doctor. Gerald saw a kitchen chair sitting next to his bed with a blanket tossed across it. He knew someone had been sitting next to his bed all night long. His father came into the room dressed, still fastening his belt. He reached down and scooped up Gerald, blankets and all and said, "Come on, sport. Doctor Roberts wants to see you. We'll get you feeling better fast." Gerald thought they must be going to give him a Speedy Alka Seltzer and he'd be "Feeling better fast." But Doctor Roberts said it was his tonsils. Gerald went to the hospital while his friends were on the Indian Guide campout. They painted the back of his throat with bad tasting medicine and wouldn't let him have any food all the next day. On Monday morning, Gerald's tonsils and adenoids came out. He didn't remember anything else about the episode except that he got to eat ice cream and Jell-O for dinner and his father brought in his crystal radio. He grounded it by fastening the alligator clip to the light next to Gerald's bed and Gerald listened to Reverend Everest and Fred Newman. That night, Fred called Gerald's house and his mother answered the phone "Hello."

◆◆◆

THE FREE CLINIC was on 8th, just across the railroad tracks. Twice G2 realized he'd turned the wrong direction and was heading away from it. He sat to rest, sleeping a while each time. When he reached the tracks, he stumbled and fell. He just lay there, thinking that if he didn't get up he'd get run over, but too exhausted to drag himself further. While he was lying there, Ben Johnson came across the tracks. G2 had ridden the rails with Ben a time once before. Ben was good company and told stories to fill the air. He seemed to accept that G2 didn't talk much and would be happiest left alone.

"Hey, G2. Ya gotta get up off the tracks, buddy," he said. He offered G2 a hand but G2 wasn't strong enough to raise his up. "You're pretty out of it today, man. Which direction you headed?" G2 raised a waved his hand vaguely toward the clinic. Ben looked that direction. "Yeah, that's a good one. Let me give you a hand." He bent down and helped G2 to his feet and supported him as they stumbled across the next set of tracks. It seemed like a long way across the yard to the clinic and there were two freight trains stopped between them and the other side. Ben led G2 down the length of one of the trains. He stopped beside a cattle car, inspected it a bit and then moved on to a box car with an open door. "This looks good," Ben said. "Better out of the wind than the cattle car. I'll bring you a bunch a straw and you'll be all set." He boosted G2's light frame up into the boxcar, shoved his feet in, and ran back to the cattle car. Before he got back, the train began to move. G2 lay huddled in a corner of the box car. He wasn't going to the clinic after all. Well, the train was a better place to die than a hospital.

◆◆◆

G2 WOKE UP IN A HOSPITAL room with five other men in beds. A tube was attached to his arm and a clear plastic bag at the other end dripped slowly into it. Some of the men snored. One tossed and rolled on his side. The man in the bed next to G2 lay flat on his back, his mouth slightly open, his eyes staring at the ceiling. So intent did that stare seem to be that G2 looked up to see what the other man saw on the ceiling. Acoustical tiles, yellow with age. G2 looked back at the man. His gaze never wavered. He never blinked. G2 had seen it before.

Uncle Al was a bus driver in a city about an hour from where Gerald lived. He had a grown son, a son about two years older than Gerald, and a daughter about the same age as Gerald's sister Marian. Gerald loved to visit Uncle Al and Aunt Millie, even though technically they weren't related to him at all. He got to ride the bus to the garage with Uncle Al. Uncle Al once gave Gerald the job of "shooting" the birds. When the starlings kept squawking in the trees outside their house, Uncle Al taught Gerald how to press a board beneath his foot and slam it on the sidewalk so it sounded like a gunshot. The starlings would all scatter and it would be quiet for about half an hour. Then they'd come back noisy as ever and Gerald would "shoot" them again. Uncle Al said he wished it was legal to use his shotgun in the city limits. He'd end the starling problem once and for all. Denny, the younger of Uncle Al's sons, had a paper route before Gerald did. He took Gerald out with him one day and it was all Gerald could do to keep up with the older boy as he sped on his route. He was following behind Denny across a street when he ran straight into the curb on the other side. Gerald flew over the handlebars and landed in the lawn. Denny said it was a good thing he didn't hit the sidewalk. The bike couldn't be ridden after that. The front wheel was caved in from the impact with the curb. Gerald was very apologetic, but Denny didn't seem to mind. "I've got another wheel in the garage," he said. Then he showed Gerald the trick of pulling up on the handlebars just before you reach a curb to lift the front wheel over. "Should have showed you that earlier," he said. It was later that year, though, that Uncle Al got sick. Gerald's family went to visit almost every weekend and took food to Aunt Millie and the kids. It seemed like everyone had something on their mind and the younger kids were left at home while the adults went to the hospital to see Uncle Al. The girls sat and played with Barbie dolls in the living room and Gerald read a book for a while. When he got bored, he wandered around the house looking at Aunt Millie's collection of salt and pepper shakers. His family always brought unique salt and peppers for Aunt Millie from wherever they traveled and apparently so did everyone else they knew. She had hundreds of pairs in glass cabinets. Gerald saw the carved cedar set his family had bought when they went to the Ozarks in the Packard. The whole store where they bought those was full of cedar carvings, including the salt and pepper that were balanced on either end of a saw sticking through the trunk of a tree, all about three inches across. Gerald had a cup and ball from that store, but his father wouldn't buy him a sling shot. The store's smell was like a closet only a hundred times more. Everything was fresh cut cedar wood. Gerald's favorite salt and pepper shakers in Aunt Millie's collection were the owls. Two brown owls held salt and pepper, but beside them were three smaller owls that were simply their family. Eventually the day came when everyone visited Uncle Al in the hospital. It was time to say goodbye, Gerald's mom told him. Is he going to die now? Gerald wanted to know. Very soon. But he wants to see everyone first. Gerald didn't know that when it was time to die you could wait until you saw everyone first. That was good to know. When it was time for him to die, he was going to think of someone who would take days or maybe years to get to him so that he could stay alive until he saw them to say goodbye. There was bad traffic that day and their car overheated. Gerald's dad had to call AAA to get help. That took a couple of hours while Gerald and his sister finally went to sleep in the back seat of the car and his mother sat with her head bowed in the front. They drove faster than his dad usually drove when they could finally get started again and arrived at the hospital just in time to see Aunt Millie come out of Uncle Al's room. Gerald's mother swept her into her arms and his father wrapped his arms around both women. Gerald peeked through the open door. Denny and his brother and sister all stood silently on the other side of the bed Uncle Al lay in with their heads bowed and tears running down their cheeks. Gerald had never seen Denny cry. Uncle Al lay on his back with his lips slightly parted, staring up at the ceiling. He didn't blink. He didn't breathe. Apparently Uncle Al couldn't wait.

◆◆◆

G2 WOKE UP THINKING. The man in the bed next to him was snoring loudly. Different man. The dead one had been replaced almost as quickly as they could change the sheets. He wondered if this was where he would die and who he should ask to see before he went. Appendix, the doctor had said. They brought a form to him and asked him name, address, and a lot of information G2 didn't know. He took the form from the doctor and wrote his name in block letters: Gerald Good, G2. He didn't have an address, didn't know if any of his relatives were living, didn't know his medical history. He dragged a disused memory from the depths of his subconscious and wrote down a social security number. He thought he remembered it right. And how old was he? 50? 52? He wrote down his birthdate, but wasn't sure if it was September or October. Well, it was close enough. Then he remembered one other thing. There wasn't a spot on the form for it, so he wrote it in the address blank. "M16-999." You never forgot your first license plate. It was still on the old Chevrolet Impala his father kept in the garage, even after he bought the new Gremlin that he died in. Some things were very clear. Others didn't seem to make any sense at all.

◆◆◆

GERALD WOKE UP that Saturday morning thinking he had to get out and make his deliveries before 6:00 a.m. He was going on seven months without a complaint or a missed collection. He was well on his way to becoming carrier of the year and winning one of the trips to Disneyland next summer. Only six trips would be awarded to the top six carriers of the year. Junior High was much more fun since Gerald got the paper route. He had a transistor radio — not the old crystal radio — that he bought with his earnings from the route. It had five bands, AM, FM, two Short Wave bands, and a Weather Band. Late at night, Gerald could tune in Quito, Ecuador on the Short Wave, and had found performances from the Grand Ole Opry in Nashville.

He got up and dressed in his long underwear, jeans, and a pair of coveralls and then pulled on the hooded parka he loved. The weather had turned bitter cold that week and with the fresh snow, there was no way he would be able to ride his fat-tired bike this morning. Once the snow had been plowed, shoveled, and packed down he could go just about anywhere on that old bike. Of course in the summer he would ride the new 5-speed Schwinn that he got for Christmas. But for hauling his heavy load of papers, there was really nothing like the big Monark with fenders, carrier rack, generator light, and shock absorbers. Both bikes would stay in the garage this morning. He pulled the twin bags over his shoulders and left through the garage, patting the big car on the hood as he stepped out into the cold. "Agent M-one-six-niner-niner-niner on assignment," he said to himself. The first bite of wind reminded him to wrap the scarf around his face. The bags were heavy, but he knew they would get lighter as he went. He fell twice before he delivered the first paper. It was going to be a long morning.

Half an hour later, tears had frozen to Gerald's cheeks. His fingers were numb, even inside the two pairs of heavy gloves he wore. His ears beneath the stocking cap and parka were burning. He wasn't even a quarter of the way through his route, slogging through the big drifts between houses. He couldn't feel his toes. Gerald turned the corner and saw his father's big Chevrolet idling in front of his next delivery. He was so thankful to see the big car that fresh tears ran down to join the ones frozen on his cheeks. He opened the passenger door and his father beckoned him. "Get in and get warm," he said. "With both of us delivering we'll get them delivered in time." Gerald shoved the bags between them on the front seat, pulled his gloves off to lay his hands directly on the heat vents. As soon as his teeth quit chattering he said softly, "Thanks, Dad." His father didn't have to get up on Saturday morning, so Gerald knew this was special. "You showed your commitment this morning, son," his father said. "I'll always be there when you are committed."

Of course, G2's father wasn't there now. He hadn't been there since a year after that morning when he crashed the new Gremlin on an icy road.

But that morning the Impala was Gerald's salvation. His father would roll to a stop in the middle of the street and the two would grab a handful of papers and jump out of each side of the car. His father took one side of the street and Gerald took the other. The newspaper publisher always gave him a lot of extra papers, so they delivered to every house, whether it was a subscriber or not. They raced each other up the block and back to the car to drive to the next block. In half an hour, Gerald was jumping out of the car to deliver the last paper on his route. That was when he slammed the door shut on his finger. His gloves were so thick and his hands so cold that for a moment Gerald thought he had only caught his glove. Then the stinging pain broke through the numbness and arced into his mind like a bolt of lightning. His scream was still echoing down the street when his father wrenched the door open, took the last paper from Gerald's hand, snapped a rubber band around it, and flung it sidearm at the last house. It clanged against the aluminum storm door. Even through the pain and tears, Gerald remembered thinking "Bullseye—way to go Dad." His dad got Gerald into the car, and they were home in ten minutes. The pain was terrible. It felt like his whole arm was going to explode. Once the garage door was down and they got into the house, Gerald's father was stripping the coat and gloves off his son to look at the damage. The ring finger was already beginning to turn an angry purple. "You're going to lose that one," his father said. Gerald cried out as a new flood of tears, this time in panic, hit him. "Not ze finger," his father laughed. "Yus ze nail." The whole family had laughed when they sat around listening to a Danny Kaye album of fairy tales. "Clever Gretel" came to mind. In order to conceal her gluttony she told the guest that the master was going to cut off both his ears. The guest fled from the house and Gretel told the master that he had stolen both chickens. The master, with knife still gripped in his hand, ran down the street after his guest screaming "Not bos, yus one!" Gerald choked back the tears to laugh at his father's imitation. He broke ice cubes out of a tray, wrapped them in a dish towel, and smashed them with a kitchen mallet. He wrapped the ice towel around Gerald's finger and Gerald winced, but was determined not to cry again. "I know it's cold and it hurts, son, but if we don't ice it will swell up so big you won't be able to put your hand through your shirtsleeve." That was terrifying, so Gerald bucked up and kept the ice in place. "You keep that on," said his father, "and by the time I get pancakes and hot chocolate made, the worst will be over." Gerald thought that was a little bit of an exaggeration. He ate aspirin with his pancakes at his mother's insistence. Later in the day, the blood had pooled beneath the nail turning it black and it hurt worse, even though Gerald had kept his hand above his head all day. His father looked at the nail before bed and decided to operate.

Gerald's father always carried a pocket knife. It was small—what some people would call a penknife, though Gerald didn't know why. It was very sharp. Gerald had watched his father hone an edge on the knife often. The knife was often called into play if someone had a splinter. His dad could use just the tip of his knife to lift a splinter right out of your hand. This time, though, his dad lit a sulfur match from beside the kitchen stove and ran it up and down the length of the knife blade. Gerald wasn't sure what his dad intended to do, but he waited patiently at the kitchen table with his injured hand palm-down, flat on the table. His father sat down beside him and touched the blade of the knife to the back of his own hand to show Gerald that the blade would not burn. Then he placed the tip gently against the center of the nail and began twisting the blade rapidly back and forth. The result was a small hole, drilled through the nail. As soon as the knife point broke through the nail, blood began to seep out through the hole and with the blood, the painful pressure. His father sopped up the blood with a cotton swab and when the bleeding slowed down he poured alcohol over the wound and put a Band-Aid on it. "I'm not really a doctor," his father intoned solemnly. "But you play one on TV," Gerald supplied. They laughed and Gerald went to bed. For the next few days, the pressure under the nail would build and Gerald's father would relieve the pressure by reopening the hole. Eventually, about three weeks later, the nail fell off and a new one began to harden beneath it.

G2 still remembered the pain in that finger. It started up again when the weather turned cold. It wasn't the acute pain of the injury, but a nagging ache, like it was doing now. Gerald strained to see out the window, over another bed in the ward where he was recovering. He wasn't sure, but it looked like it was snowing.

◆◆◆

"MR. GOOD, I'M MR. STANLEY, your social worker. The doctors tell me that you are healed up enough to leave the hospital now, but we have to have somewhere to take you. We can't turn you out of the hospital and onto the streets, especially in this weather. So I've arranged a stay in a halfway house for you. You won't need to do any work for the next two weeks, but as soon as the doctor says you are fit, they'll send you out on light jobs to help pay for the housing and food. You need to stay clean and sober during your stay. This is a great opportunity for you to get healthy. You might find a way to turn your life around with this little incident. You are lucky to be alive."

The weather Mr. Stanley was talking about included at least a foot of new snow that Gerald gazed at out the front window of Mr. Stanley's car as they drove to the halfway house. The social worker drove a small foreign car and G2 could bet that didn't make him popular among out-of-work autoworkers. Just across the bridge they were passing, was Canada. G2 didn't think Canada had many homeless people. The winters would kill them off. He wasn't sure how he got to Detroit but assumed the train Ben Johnson had dumped him on was northbound instead of southbound. Trust Ben to send him into a frozen hell. Maybe that had saved his life, though. The yardmaster in Detroit had called an ambulance when he found G2. Would they have done that in Mobile?

Mr. Stanley led G2 into the halfway house to meet the manager, Bob Brown. Bob told G2 where to sleep – in a room with three single beds – when he could shower, and what time to sit down at the table for dinner. He laid down strict rules. There would be no alcohol in the house and if the resident was found to be intoxicated he would be placed on probation. A second violation would result in termination of the resident's stay. G2 would be excused from maintenance except that of his personal area for the first two weeks at the doctor and social worker's request. He would still be required to attend one of the two 12-step meetings held in the house each day. While he was recovering, G2 should work jigsaw puzzles, crossword puzzles, read the newspaper, read a bock a week, and help around the house as he could. There would be no harm in his sweeping or running the vacuum cleaner, and the manager was sure he could do dishes within a day or two.

"I'm Bob Brown and I'm an alcoholic," the manager said by way of introducing the first 12-step meeting. "Hello Bob," responded all the men in the house. "I've been sober 7 months, 2 days, and 18 hours and there isn't one hour of that time that I haven't been tempted to find a bottle," Bob said. He asked G2 to introduce himself. G2 struggled to get words to come out of his mouth. They all expected him to say "I'm Gerald Good and I'm an alcoholic." They would all respond "Hello Gerald," and he wouldn't know who they were talking to. He'd left Gerald behind years ago. There was no one left but G2. The words simply wouldn't come out of his mouth and tears began running down his cheeks from the effort. Manager Bob laid a hand on G2's shoulder and told him that the hand of God was on him, casting out the demons of alcohol and his old life. They were all there to help G2 get through this hard time and he could sit down and take his time. G2 breathed an almost silent "God bless," and sat back down sobbing. He didn't know what happened during the rest of the meeting, but by the end, G2 had been paired with a kind black man who simply sat with him and said he was G2's sponsor. Together they'd help each other find victory over the bottle and salvation in the love of God. Amen.

G2 was in prison. His sponsor, Muhammad "Go-Lightly" Jones, was pleasant company. He'd been in the halfway house for six weeks and sat with G2 while they worked the unending jigsaw puzzles. They went to meetings together and sat to eat together. But they never left the house. G2 could not leave the house unless he was accompanied by either Manager Bob or his social worker, Mr. Stanley. He kept his little canvas bag with him all the time, in case he was allowed to leave, but neither man saw a reason for him to go out, so G2 sat quietly in the house and thought as he looked out the window at the mounting snow.

◆◆◆

GERALD HAD NEVER SEEN so much snow as that winter when he was nine. The winds blew in off the lake and dumped foot upon foot of snow in his community. School was closed for two weeks and there was talk of extending the school year into the summer if the snow didn't clear soon. Gerald was only four feet tall, but the snow drifts were twice his height or more. Cars sat buried along the street and the one time a snowplow came down the middle of the road it piled the drifts against the cars even higher. The good part was that Brian's mother brought him by Gerald's house and the two stayed together for the next five days. Once the snow stopped, it stayed cold, but was bright and sunny. The boys were dressed in snowsuits and sent outside. It was a different world. The sun warmed just enough during the day to melt the top layer of snow which then froze during the long cold night. As a result, they could walk along on top of the drifts if they were careful. They sledded down the street and ran into the snow banks on either side. It was truly a winter wonderland.

But the best was when Brian broke through the ice and plummeted down into a drift. He was up to his shoulders and each time the boys tried to get him out, a new chunk of ice would break at the surface. That was when the "great idea" came to him. Gerald ran to get the coal shovel from the garage. About ten feet away from Brian, he broke through the side of a drift and began shoveling out the snow inside the drift. Brian used his mittened hands to scoop and pack the snow to the side as he tunneled toward Gerald. It was a near disaster when the shovel broke through the last membrane of snow between the boys and almost hit Brian in the head, but they had discovered the joy of having a snow tunnel. The sunlight filtered through the ice and snow above them making the tunnel alive with a diffuse light. Brian and Gerald were explorers in a strange new alien world where a soccer ball left outside before the snow started became a rare life form discovered as they conquered their snow-planet. They didn't need to remove much of the snow from the tunnels they dug over the next few days. Mostly they could pack it down on the floors and walls of the tunnel. The snow that they removed, they packed into a box that they moved on the sled dragged into the tunnel behind them. The cubes of snow dumped out of the box made the walls of an elaborate snow fort with crenulated parapets and a tower with real ice block stairs. They even tunneled between two snowbound cars and broke an opening through to the street. Mr. Harmon had not been happy when the snow melted enough to get his car out and he found shovel scratches along one side where the boys had run into it and then tunneled along it to find the gap between cars.

That winter was the best winter of Gerald's life. Even when the snow started to melt and their ice cave ceilings fell in, the maze of tunnels stayed and were great for playing tag or their own warped version of fox and geese.

◆◆◆

G2 HATED WINTER NOW. Snow outside meant that he had to find shelter and shelter meant no wine. Shelter also meant closed spaces with men snoring and farting through the night. Staying inside meant long hours with nothing to occupy his time but thinking. And that's what prison was. Having to be all alone with the thoughts in his head.

He tried to follow the advice of Manager Bob and work jigsaw puzzles. He swept the floors every day. He had spent hours with a crossword puzzle, but when Manager Bob saw the neatly penned license numbers filling every square in the grid and the underlined words in the clues he told G2 it would be better if he left the crosswords to some of the other men. G2 vowed to himself to escape or die trying. He only needed to wait for his opportunity.

It came ten days later. Mr. Stanley picked up G2 to go to the hospital to get his stitches out. G2 planned everything ahead. His little bag stayed packed. There wasn't much in it anymore, but he didn't want to be seen stuffing things into it just before he left the house. When Mr. Stanley arrived, G2 pulled his bag over his shoulder and put the army surplus overcoat on right over the top of it. He signed out of the house under the house manager's watchful eye and Mr. Stanley signed as escort. They would be gone no more than two hours and G2 was expected to sign back in. The doctor at the hospital examined G2's appendix incision and snipped the end of the staple that held him together while the operation healed. "Treat it gently for a few days, G2," the doctor said. "You should be back to your old self within a week." The doctor went out to talk to Mr. Stanley who was in the waiting room. G2 pulled his hat and coat on, shouldered his bag and left before they returned. It took him a while to find the freight yard. He had to make sure he wasn't spotted by Mr. Stanley driving around looking for him. But curled up in the army surplus coat in the back of a boxcar, G2 left Detroit on a southbound train.

◆◆◆

G2 LIKED BEING SOUTH in the winter. It wasn't like it was never cold. But what sent the locals running for sweaters and overcoats felt like a spring breeze to G2. He didn't plan to stay in this particular town for long, but the train had run out of track when it reached the ocean, so he had to find the necessities of life and then find a way out of town. His path took him through the Historic District. G2 was tired and weak. He hadn't had food since… He couldn't remember exactly. His bottle and the loaf of bread had run out on the train. A big sign near the river said "No panhandling." Bums seemed to be ignoring the sign as they approached people asking for a couple of bucks, sometimes even grabbing hold of a sleeve if a passerby ignored them. These were people that G2 didn't want to be involved with. He turned south on Whitaker and saw a man give two dollars to a woman selling flowers. Half a block further, the man dropped the flower on the sidewalk. G2 picked up the flower and caught up with the man to return it to him. "Oh for Christ's sake. Get lost. I already donated. Come any closer and I'll call the cops." The man continued on his way leaving G2 with the flower in his hand. It wasn't a real flower. It was made of straw or reeds. G2 recalled that some of the homeless who camped over near Tybee Island cut the reeds and fashioned them into roses, then others sold them for a living. It was delicate — beautiful in its own way.

Of course, Gerald knew roses. His mother loved them. Gerald kept his paper route until he was a sophomore in high school and one of the things he did with his money was join the Rose of the Month Club so that he could plant roses for his mother. She was so sad after his father died. There were two bedraggled rose bushes in the back yard and in spite of their lack of care (and the number of times they'd kicked a football into them), his mother would sit at the kitchen table looking out into the back yard in the spring and stare at the blossoms. Gerald read up on the care of roses and joined the club, determined that he would make a rose garden that would match the White House. During the spring and summer, he received his monthly rose bush in the mail and read the instructions for care and planting. Then he dug a spot in the back yard and planted it. Come November, the instructions changed. The dormant plants received in the mail were to be hung in a cool dry place until the ground thawed in the spring and then planted. Gerald hung the five winter roses from hooks in the garage and hoped it didn't get so cold that they plants died. Winter care for the roses that were planted had been difficult. Thanksgiving weekend, even though there was already snow on the ground, Gerald went out to the rose bed, pruned, and trenched his roses. This amounted to cutting them back impossibly far, then loosening the dirt around the roots and laying the rose plants over on their sides. Then he covered the plants with newspaper and straw to protect them during the winter. The job took him all day on Friday after Thanksgiving. He had even pruned and trenched the two straggly plants that had been there before he started his project. He had prepared his rose bed the previous spring by building a raised bed out of old 2x4s that he buried an inch deep and filled the inside with fill dirt from a home construction site that was being dug a block away from his house. In spite of warnings from the neighbors about the composition of the soil and the inadvisability of digging a basement, the contractor had dug out a full basement for the new home, so Gerald had carted away all the top soil he could in his wheelbarrow and filled a bed 12 feet long and six feet wide in the back yard. The basement of the new house was poured concrete and the framing was up when the first big thunderstorm hit that spring. After the storms, the builder had returned to find the basement cracked and flooded. Sage neighbors had wagged their heads and commented about too much clay for a basement, an underground river, and quicksand under the town. Gerald didn't know how much of what the neighbors had said was true, but he did have dreams about the whole town being slowly sucked into the ground because of the quicksand underneath. The builder didn't return that summer and the site stood derelict through the winter, framed studs standing like stark bones of a house that would never be built. The city eventually condemned the place and bulldozers came in to remove all sign of human habitation, which meant taking away all the building supplies and filling in the basement. Gerald couldn't remember that a house had ever been built on that lot before he left for college.

In the spring, Gerald uncovered his roses as soon as the snow had melted off the straw. He stood them upright and gently packed the soil around their roots. He planted the five winter roses and then cancelled his membership in the Rose of the Month Club. There was no room for more than the 14 roses he now had in his garden. By Easter, all of the roses had leafed out and sent new shoots up to the welcoming sunlight and by June the buds had appeared on the bushes. Gerald watched his mother fix her coffee and sit at the kitchen table each morning looking out at the rose bushes and the riot of colors that they bloomed in. Gerald had not planned the garden by color, but rather by the month of the delivery. There were yellow roses next to pink next to white next to red. They bloomed all summer long and until Gerald left college and started wandering the country, he returned every Thanksgiving to prune and trench the roses and each spring break to set them upright again.

G2 wondered, as he looked at the Savannah rose in his hand if the roses were still there. Did anyone care for them? Were they all as straggly as those first two had been, or were they all dead by now?

Sometimes when G2 smelled fresh coffee, he had a fleeting glimpse of his mother at the kitchen table flit through his mind. She had loved the roses.

◆◆◆

A KIND PERSON at Sweet Charlotte's saw G2 hanging around the back door, looking to see if there had been any slices of pizza thrown in the garbage. He was almost faint with hunger and his head complained of having had no wine. Sometimes the garbage behind a restaurant was not too bad. More and more, they were dumping things down garbage disposals at restaurants, though. He might have better luck at a grocery store, but couldn't think where there was one just at the moment. A woman in an apron appeared at the back door shaking a cigarette out of a pack as she opened the door with her shoulder. She had spiky hair and tattoos that ran up her left arm. The inside of each wrist was tattooed with a Chinese character. Half a dozen earrings hung from each ear and there was a hoop stuck through her eyebrow and another through her nose. She looked tough, but Gerald thought she was strangely pretty. She looked up at him as she emerged from the kitchen. "Hey, you!" The voice wasn't sharp, but G2 shied away nonetheless. He was used to being shooed away from places and found it best to just go. "Don't go," the woman said. "Come here. You hungry?" G2 nodded his head. "Wait." She went back inside and came out a moment later with a paper plate and three slices of pizza. "Here. Sit down and eat. I like company when I come out to smoke." G2 sat on the step at her feet and savored the pizza. It was cold — not refrigerator cold, but cold like it had been sitting out for a while. "You're new around here, aren't you?" G2 nodded, his mouth full of pizza. "If I have leftovers you're welcome to them. People leave so much food on their plates it's a shame to waste it. When they leave slices of pizza, I stack them up and hand 'em out if people need something to eat. Better than throwing it in the garbage. That one's the specialty of the house. Enough calories in one slice to keep a normal man going for a week. Three meats and three cheeses and guaranteed to give you greasy farts all night long. Can't believe guys bring their dates here and then think they'll get lucky later on. I'm vegetarian myself. I eat pizza, but just with tomato sauce and vegetables on it. My own specialty. I'll save a piece for you tomorrow night." She finished her cigarette about the same time G2 finished the last slice of pizza. He turned to her and said "God bless." "Don't worry, She will," the woman responded. "Now how about you help me out a little. I haven't had time to get out front and clean things up. Take this broom out and sweep the walks in front of the restaurant nice and clean. Pick up the trash and put it in the can out there, don't just sweep it into the street. Bring the broom back here when you're done and I'll give you a couple bucks." G2 took the broom and dustpan and hurried to the front to sweep the walks. He was happy to repay the woman's kindness.

◆◆◆

G2 KNEW HOW TO SWEEP. He learned from a pro. G2 called him Mr. Bags in his head, but had never heard his name spoken. He wore the baggiest pair of pants G2 had ever seen on a skinny man. Mr. Bags said they fit him just fine before he went on his diet. Mr. Bags showed up at the local coffee shop about 11:30 every day with his broom. The broom was worn down to little more than a stub, but it worked just fine on the cement sidewalk. He would politely and carefully begin at the crack in the sidewalk coinciding with where the coffee shop adjoined the upscale restaurant next door. Mr. Bags never swept in front of the restaurant. "They got people who do that," Mr. Bags would say. "I don't want to take anybody's work away from them, even though they don't do a very good job." He pointed out the bits of trash in the gutter. Each night after closing, the restaurant sent one of their busboys outside with a hose that he hooked to the faucet and used a special wrench to turn on. He sprayed from the front of the restaurant out to the street, sweeping all the accumulated day worth of gum wrappers and mint papers and occasional pile of dog poop out into the street. There he left it, assuming that it would get washed down the gutters or a street sweeper would come by in the middle of the night and vacuum the crap up. Mr. Bags, however, was meticulous. He swept carefully, one section of sidewalk at a time from the building to the curb. But he didn't sweep the detritus off the walk. He used a piece of cardboard, swept the trash onto it and deposited it in the receptacle outside the coffee shop. Then he moved to the next section of sidewalk and swept it. The piece of corrugated that Mr. Bags used as a dustpan was his sign. It read: "Not poor. Just can't afford food. Thanks for helping." It was a lot of words, G2 thought, but people often struggled to read the sign while Mr. Bags used it to catch a batch of dirt and paper. The other side of the sign read "Tips appreciated." That way no matter what side of the sign people saw, they got the message. Those who read always seemed to have a dollar or two for Mr. Bags.

It wasn't just sweeping. Mr. Bags had carefully instructed G2 on how to sweep properly, how to wait for a section to clear of customers before attempting to sweep it, and how to make sure his sign was always face up. Mr. Bags also acted as a sort of unofficial busboy. If he saw people finish at a sidewalk table and stand to leave, he politely asked them if he could take their paper cups and dishes for them. He would hold his sign in one hand like a waiter's tray and put the trash on it. Customers often put a dollar or some change on the table which Mr. Bags picked up as he was cleaning. "It's all about customer service," Mr. Bags said. Some people said that Mr. Bags had once been a waiter in a fancy restaurant. Some even said it was the restaurant next door. Why he had become a street sweeper, though, no one knew and Mr. Bags didn't say. He would disappear from about 2:00 until 5:00 when he would once again be at his appointed station. On nights when the theatre across the street had performances, he would often stay late, sweeping the sidewalk in front of the coffee shop even though it was closed. People leaving one of the restaurants nearby and hurrying to the theatre sometimes left him a little something on one of the tables. People with doggy bags from their restaurant seemed prone to realize that they couldn't take the food into the theatre with them and left that.

One day, Mr. Bags didn't show up at the coffee shop. There were questions asked and genuine concern on the part of both patrons and employees. Mr. Bags was found in the small orange tent he occupied in Tent City II. He'd died in his sleep. A local church held a memorial service and the coffee shop donated half their proceeds for the day to a homeless shelter. More than a hundred people came to Mr. Bags' funeral. The newspaper published a story about him and as much of his history as they could find. The coffee shop hung Mr. Bags' cardboard sign on the trashcan outside the shop and after about a year they replaced it with a real brass plaque next to the door. It said simply, "Thanks for helping."

No one had taken up the job of sweeping the sidewalk after Mr. Bags died.

◆◆◆

WITH THE THREE DOLLARS he'd gotten from Sweet Charlotte, G2 managed to get a bottle of wine and was settling down next to a park bench to enjoy a sip. It was full dark and most people had left the park. This bench was a bit out of the way and no street lights illuminated it. Rather than sit on the bench, G2 sat down beside it and leaned against the seat. He looked once again at the reed rose he held in his hand. It didn't seem right to just throw it away. He took a mouthful of wine and let it sit on his tongue while he contemplated the matter. The wine was a little sour, but at $3.50 a bottle G2 wasn't expecting Cabernet Sauvignon. G2 doubted that he ever got drunk on wine. It seemed he never had enough to be drunk, but as the wine warmed on his tongue a deep peace settled in over him. It was a clear night and he would sleep beneath the stars with a rose on his chest. Perhaps he would have no dreams.

It was into this peaceful state of bliss that the woman hurrying through the park with a slight limp on her left side tripped over G2. He nearly choked, swallowing the wine in his mouth. "Oh, I'm so sorry!" she said. "Are you all right?" Not from here, G2 thought. A Northerner like himself, come south to get warm. That gave him a sudden idea. He nodded his head and held out the rose to her. She pulled back instinctively from his outstretched hand, but then approached and took the flower. "That's beautiful," she said wistfully. "You must be an artist." G2 didn't want to take credit for the flower's craftsmanship, but he still had a bit of wine in his mouth and didn't want to say anything. She seemed to get the message and sat on the bench next to where he sat on the ground. She exuded confidence. G2 would have guessed she was much younger, but her appearance in the dim light suggested a woman, maybe as old as he was. He couldn't remember right away how old that was. He had been 50 a while back, but he didn't remember if that was last year or a few years ago. She searched in her purse for a moment and produced a ten dollar bill and handed it to him. Ten dollars! She didn't immediately get up and rush away, though. G2 listened as she rambled on. "You get to be whoever you want to be and no one tells you to be someone else. I know life must be hard for you and I don't mean to romanticize it, but I've often wondered what it would be like to be truly free of everyone's expectations and just leave everything behind. But there is so much to give up; I know I couldn't do it. There's my friends, of course. It is so painful to lose a friend and sit through their funeral and say goodbye forever. How could I ever inflict that pain on them and just leave. And security. Having a home, a dog, a job. Those are the things that define me." G2 noticed she didn't say a husband. He bet she was just as alone as he was when it came down to it. He dared another sip from his bottle and offered it to her. "No, you enjoy it. I'm afraid I can't. That's what life is about — what I can't do, not what I can do. If you don't have anything, is it easier to give up what you have?" She was silent a moment and G2 sat looking expectantly at her. Then she rose and turned away.

"God bless," G2 said softly. She hesitated a moment as if snared by his words, but she didn't turn back. She hurried on her way.

◆◆◆

GERALD WAS DOWN to his last marble. He hadn't had many to start with — a set of ten cat-eyes and a shooter that the kids called a boulder. Lots of the kids had marbles and they spent their time during recess trying to win them from each other. Gerald's mother had taught him how to draw a circle in the sand and put the small marbles in the middle. Then he learned how to use his thumb to flick the shooter out of his fingers to hit the center marbles. He'd become rather good at knocking a marble out of the circle with the shooter. But the kids at school didn't play that way. One kid tossed a marble out on the ground about eight feet away. The second would stand in the same place and throw his marble at the target. If he hit it, he won the marble. If he missed, the first shooter stood with a toe where his own marble had landed and try to hit the second kid's target. This continued until someone hit a marble and won the match and the marble. Gerald wasn't good at this game. It hadn't taken long before he had lost all his cat-eye marbles and had only his boulder left. He hung on to the big marble, afraid to take a challenge or to make one. He watched everyone else play. That wasn't as much fun as playing, even if he lost. Finally, Gerald put his boulder into play against a tough kid who had a big bag of marbles. Gerald tossed his marble out and held his breath as the other boy lined up to take his shot. If he lost, Gerald would no longer have any marbles. He was so anxious to have a bag of marbles rattling at his side again that his heart was beating too fast and his breath was coming in little gasps. The second marble was in the air, a long arcing flight that landed just short of Gerald's marble, bounced and struck it solidly. Gerald watched his last marble being collected by the other boy. His gasping short breath must have sounded like sobs because the other boy said, "Gees, don't cry. It's just a marble." But rather than give it back, the boy pocketed it, turned, and walked away.

Gerald was shocked, but relieved at the same time. The competition was over. He was out. He didn't have any marbles, but it didn't seem to make any difference. It's not like the marbles were valuable. For a dollar he could buy another bag. He wasn't even sure that he liked marbles. They just happened to be what everyone was doing. And now that he didn't have any, he didn't really care. He'd always liked swinging, but he didn't have to own a swing. Even if he liked marbles, he didn't have to own any. He didn't have to put them away, or risk them, or lose them, or win them. In fact, a stone that he picked up was just about the same as a marble. Maybe it wasn't as perfectly round, but you could play the same game and there wouldn't be any tears wasted or gloating done based on winning or losing. Marbles were really kind of silly.

◆◆◆

G2 HID behind a batch of railroad ties stacked up on the near side of the switch yard. He'd barely managed to snatch up his blanket and bag before he ran from the little camp. There were only a dozen men sleeping under the overpass tonight, but tonight of all times the police had decided to close down camps all over the city. Lights shone on the remaining men scrambling to clean up their tents. Police were shouting instructions to leave the cardboard boxes and get in the van. They'd be taken to a shelter and social workers would help them in the morning. The men filed onto the bus solemnly. Two policemen with a dog walked through the remains of the camp shining a flashlight into boxes and a lean-to made of brush, kicking the fire out, and shaking a blanket that had been left. Then a bulldozer moved forward and scraped all sign of human inhabitation off the ground and into a dump truck. The van pulled away and headed onto the ramp for the southbound freeway. Whatever shelter the men were headed for, it wasn't inside the city limits, G2 guessed. The floodlights were dismantled, and packed away. The police got back in their cars. The bulldozer was loaded onto a flatbed truck and everyone drove away. The whole operation had taken less than an hour and they were off to clear another camp.

People assumed that if there were no places in town for the homeless to sleep, then they would no longer stay in town. But it didn't work that way. Tomorrow the men would meet up with men and women from other camps. They would talk together in hushed tones. Some would say they were headed to San Francisco. Others would say they were staying. Someone would mention an abandoned warehouse they discovered big enough for a hundred. People would nod their heads.

The shelters would "process" them. Name? Last permanent residence? How long homeless? Skills? Need for medical attention? Education? Family? A few were good at this and would ask for assisted living. One or two would plead disabilities. Some would make sure the shelter lost track of them. Late that night, there would be three or four people prying open the door of an abandoned warehouse. The next night a dozen would have staked out places to sleep. In a week, there could be a hundred. The police would debate whether to move them out, but no one could locate the owner who would have to file a complaint. A councilman would suggest that the city should let them have the warehouse. Another would suggest it might get burned down.

But the homeless would still be in the city. The "problem" wouldn't be solved. Days, weeks, or maybe months later, the whole scenario would be repeated, by which time the overpass would have a dozen men living in boxes under it.

G2 didn't have a box. He didn't have much in his bag, and aside from the fact that he had a bottle he wouldn't have missed the bag that much. He could rewrite the license numbers in his little book by heart because he read them every night. The weather was warm enough not to really need a blanket. He didn't have much, so he couldn't lose much. He took the smallest sip from his bottle and slept with his back against the pile of railroad ties, a hundred yards from where the camp had been destroyed. He would be on the first train that moved in the morning.

◆◆◆

THE TRAIN WAS SITTING on the siding when the sun came up. G2 awoke and moved from his cramped quarters beneath the V of the hopper. There was a scent of newly mown hay in the air that had invaded his dreams all morning. There was no telling how long the train would sit on the siding. It could still be there tomorrow at this time. Across the fields, G2 could see activity in a farmyard.

◆◆◆

YOU DIDN'T HAVE TO GO FAR outside of town to be in open farm-land where Gerald grew up. Gerald had friends who lived on farms and he spent his share of time in the country. The best time was hay-ing season. There was so much to smell and so much work to do. When he was baling hay, or more likely walking behind the tractor tossing bales up onto the hay wagon, he felt good, like he was accom-plishing something. You could see the results. His mom still insisted on asking him each day after school what he learned. By the time Gerald was 17, she had become used to hearing "I don't know. Stuff." It wasn't that Gerald didn't learn in school. He was a good student. But how did you quantify what you learned? It didn't make sense. He wanted to tell her that he'd filled 14,372 brain cells with information and created 27,000 new synapses. Then she would know he learned something. You just couldn't recite everything that happened during the day and point to it and say "This is what I learned." But hay bales were a different thing. Different entirely. The flat bed of the wagon held 40 bales on the bottom three tiers. Then they narrowed in to 32 bales on the next three tiers. The top two tiers held 16 bales each before they threw a tarp over the whole lot and strapped it down. 238 bales per wagonload. It was eight tenths of a mile to the barn to unload the wagon. All the time the baler was continuing to work its way through the field. Gerald and three friends raced to stack the hay in the barn and then drive back to the field, hoping against hope that they would be able to catch up to the relentless march of the baler, now over 300 bales ahead of them. Two boys would walk alongside the wagon tossing bales up onto the flatbed from either side. One boy on top of the wagon was the stacker and had to make sure they were packed tightly and securely. Junior, the farmer's son, drove the tractor down between the rows of bales as fast as the boys could keep up. 238 bales and they headed back to the barn. By the time they got back the baler would be another 300 bales ahead of them. By nightfall, they would be exhausted, but would spray themselves off with a cold hose and drag themselves into the farmhouse where Mrs. Levinson had dinner waiting for them. They were almost too tired to eat, but too hungry not to. Gerald would drive home, fighting to stay awake, thinking of nothing but his bed. His mother never asked, "How many bales did you stack today?" One thousand nine hundred and four, thank you. The question was always the same. "What did you learn today?" what did Gerald learn, baling hay? The next morning, before sunrise, he would be back in the field, arms and back so sore that they couldn't move as fast that day, but farmer Levinson was finished baling that field so he drove the tractor and Junior had to help stack. When Junior stacked he could get 270 bales per load. 2,420 bales for the day and the field was all stacked. Farmer Levinson's barn was so big that the more than 4,000 bales from that field didn't half fill it. At an average of 80 pounds per bale, the boys stacked 160 tons of hay in two days. Hay was important. Each of Mr. Levinson's Holsteins would need 30 pounds or more of hay a day during the winter to keep them milking. He'd start supplementing pasturage even before the first snow fell. Figuring 160 feeding days for 200 milk cows, meant that over 480 tons of hay would be needed to last the winter. Each successive cutting would yield less hay until the fourth cutting, if they could get one in before snowfall, would yield only about 80 tons. They would need every bale stacked up in the barn by the end of the winter. But why ask what he learned? He knew exactly how much hay he stacked.

♦♦♦

IT WAS DIFFERENT THESE DAYS, G2 thought. He rode on the hay wagon into the field and was already sweating. He'd left his bag at the farmhouse and was just a little worried about getting back to it, but work in the sun for $20 a day, food, and a barn to sleep in was good. Fast, back-breaking work in the sun was almost as good as a bottle of wine for keeping thoughts out of your head. But the work was different than when he was a kid. No one made square bales these days. The seven foot tall round bales weighed five hundred pounds each. The farmer's son drove the hay wagon tractor stopping and starting every hundred feet. The farmer drove a fork-lift through the ragged field and lifted the bale up to the wagon. G2s job was to secure it before the wagon moved so the bale wouldn't roll off the back. The work wasn't as impossibly hard as when he was a kid, but it was more dangerous. A bale rolling over the top of a man could crush him.

The wagon was about the same size that G2 remembered from his youth, but 38 bales anchored well to the wagon weighed nine and a half tons. The same that they used to get from 230 square bales. They loaded faster so the wagon made twice the trips to the field in a day. Three men in one day did the work of five in two days when G2 was a boy. He felt as good when he finished as he had after a day of stacking. Dirty, exhausted, hungry. He doused himself with a hose running cold water and was shown to a spot in the barn where he could sleep for the night He got a big plate of meat and potatoes and a bottle of water. After being admonished not to smoke, he slept deeply. The farmer's dog came into the barn and sniffed G2 up and down, then curled up next to him and slept as well. The farm, the dog, and the hay always reminded G2 not to be a dog in the manger.

♦♦♦

GERALD HAD BEEN FIGHTING with his first girlfriend. It was silly. They were nine years old. They'd grown up next door to each other and were in the same grade at school. In fact, the first day in first grade the teacher seated the class in alphabetical order. Nicki cried because she couldn't sit beside Gerald. Everyone else in the classroom was new and strange and Nicki wanted the familiarity of her friend. Once they had spent an entire afternoon bouncing on Nicki's bed — something Gerald was not allowed to do at home. "No more monkeys jumping on the bed," his mother would have said. But Nicki's mother simply warned them not to put holes in the ceiling and let them jump. It was almost as good as a trampoline.

Nicki was tiny for her age — even reflected in her full name, Nicolette — and Gerald was only slightly taller, but they were fierce competitors when it came to bicycle polo. The neighborhood kids had invented the sport which they played in the Brown's long, gravel driveway. Only six could play because that was all the mallets there were in old croquet set Mrs. Brown gave them to play with. There were only three balls with colored stripes that matched the stripes on the mallet heads, though, so the kids couldn't really play croquet unless there were only three of them to play. But they could divide up into teams of three each, drop a ball in the middle of the driveway and race at each other on their banana-seat bicycles to see who could knock the ball through the opposing team's goal. No one who fell or got scraped up on the gravel ever cried, even if they were picking cinders out of their elbows the rest of the day. No one wanted to lose the privilege of playing.

Which is why it was so strange that Nicki and Gerald were fighting over such a silly thing as the color mallet each would have. Gerald insisted that he couldn't play unless he used the blue mallet and Nicki countered that it wasn't fair for him to have the blue mallet every time. She was right, of course, but Gerald was somehow disconnected from what was right and what was wrong. All he could see was that he needed the blue mallet. Into this fray, Gerald's father walked. "Gerald, it's time to go," he said. "Go where?" Gerald demanded. "To Dowagiac to see Aunt Helen," his father reminded him. "Did you forget we aren't going to be home this weekend?" Gerald had forgotten. Suddenly the color of the mallet was irrelevant in light of the fact that he wouldn't be playing. Nicki stuck out her tongue at him and Gerald just grabbed hold harder on the mallet. "I'll take it with me so nothing happens to it," he said. His father assessed the situation quickly and knelt beside the two children. He didn't attempt to take the mallet from either of the children. "Seems that maybe you are being a bit of a dog in a manger." Both kids looked at his father with puzzled expressions. "There was once a dog that, upon entering a barn, saw a manger filled with fresh hay. 'This is a fine manger,' said the dog, 'and a good bed of fresh hay. I'll sleep here.' But no matter how many times the dog turned around on top of the hay the manger was too small for him to comfortably lie down in. This made the dog very angry. A cow came into the barn and approached the manger. 'Farmer has put my food in the manger,' the cow said. 'I'm very hungry and would like you to move, friend dog, so that I can eat my dinner.' But the dog refused to move and when the cow approached the manger to eat, the dog growled and bit at the cow until the cow went away to forage for grass outside. The dog finally grew tired of the manger in which he could not sleep and didn't want to guard anymore. He finally left and the cow ate her dinner. But their friendship had been destroyed and they never spoke to each other again. From then on, a person who growls to protect something he has no use for has been called a dog in the manger.' Gerald released the mallet and sheepishly smiled at Nicki. "Hope you win the game," he said. She grinned back as she took the mallet. As they went through school and each made more friends, they grew apart and Nicki moved to a different town in sixth grade. Gerald still thought fondly of her and hoped she had won.

◆◆◆

G2 TURNED ON HIS BED OF STRAW with the dog warming his back and smelled the sweet smell of the fresh hay. *Don't be a dog in a manger*, he thought.

The farmer had kindly given him four five-dollar bills instead of a twenty, and warned G2 that his neighbor had been known not to pay itinerant help. G2 nodded his head and said "God bless." In the morning, before the farmer had come out of the kitchen, G2 was gone. The scent of hay in the fields early in the morning carried him on the road until he reached a railroad crossing at the edge of town.

G2 examined the tracks carefully. They were worn with occasional rust marks, but not too shiny. When you looked at a railroad track, you had to determine if it was used first, and then how fast the trains went when they crossed that spot. If the train went through the town without slowing down, it was no good waiting for the train. A train couldn't be going more than 15 miles an hour to safely dive into an open cattle car or grab hold of the ladder on a coal tender. G2 had once managed a train he estimated was going 20 miles per hour, but he was much younger then. If the tracks were too shiny, the trains went too fast.

In the smaller towns that dotted the Midwestern countryside, the thing that G2 looked for was a grain elevator. Most trains that stopped to load up the big grain tankers also carried boxes or flatbeds. You selected the car in advance, but stayed well back away from the tracks until you heard the train start to move. Then you ran for the door or the flatcar and dove on. G2 didn't like flatcars much. They were windy and cold. The same was true of cattle cars, though you could usually get a bit of warmth in a cattle car by covering yourself with straw. The best were boxcars. They were enclosed, and they were dark. It wasn't easy to see someone in the corner of a boxcar even when you looked quickly with a flashlight. The biggest problem with boxcars was getting locked in. G2 was once in a train yard when the conductor started slamming the door on one side of the boxcar closed. G2 dove out the door on the other side and was across the next set of tracks before the conductor had ducked under the car to close the other door. He was chased off the tracks and out of the switch yard. But boxcars had gradually been supplanted over the 50s and 60s by standardized container cars. The articulated well cars would hold as many as four of the containers that could be lifted off and loaded individually on a sixteen wheeler. They came off the cargo ships where they were stacked as high as a seven story building. But that meant boxcars were hardly ever seen on the tracks anymore.

◆◆◆

MRS. FITES had read *The Boxcar Children* to Gerald's fourth grade class. They were too big to take an afternoon nap, but when the children came into the classroom after lunch and recess, Mrs. Fites required that everyone put their heads down on their arms at their desk while she read a chapter of the book. A lot of kids slept, and occasionally Gerald would doze off as well. But the images of four children on their own, living in a boxcar had filled his mind and excited his imagination. When they moved to the island, Gerald was certain that they would be castaway forever. Or was that a different book? Somehow, all the stories became one when Gerald and Brian played pretend games on the playground. They'd been adventurers, sailors, pilots, and heroes of their own devising. Gerald had begun writing a story of his own that year. It was an exciting adventure in which he and Brian were princes and best friends who rode matching white horses. Their adventure was to be with two young princesses of a neighboring kingdom. But Gerald got bogged down in the spelling difference between princes and princess and princesses and had left a lot of blanks on the first page of the story where one or another of the words would go. That wasn't very inspiring, and by the end of page two, Gerald had abandoned the story to write about moon exploration and spaceships. There was a dinosaur civilization in there somewhere, and he had to live in a boxcar. The stories never seemed to get more than a page or two before he started on a different one that was even more exciting. By the end of fourth grade, Gerald had foregone writing in favor of drawing. He wasn't very good at drawing things. But he could devise intricate patterns on the paper. His favorite was the five-sided curved object with each shape connected at one point with another. He would fill a page with them and then carefully fill in the space between the shapes with ink. He also like drawing mazes, but most of them either had a path that went straight through with no options that went more than an inch from the path, or a maze that had no way through at all. Once again, Gerald would fill the space on the page that wasn't in a path with ink, just to see the pattern it would make. Paper and pens and pencils. Gerald hoarded them and always had a drawer full of them in his room.

◆◆◆

THERE WERE NO TRAINS on the siding at the grain elevator and only a few empty hoppers. There was no telling how long it would be before a train came through, nor if it would stop. He walked along a backstreet parallel to the highway, watching to avoid police. The street came up along the back of a truck stop. G2 headed for the store, bought a tuna salad sandwich and a bottle of wine. Then he headed to the parking lot to eat and have a sip. While he waited, he heard the whistle blow as a train approached the town's one gated crossing. G2 headed for the road, but the train did not slow enough to run across the road and hop aboard.

He waited in the parking lot and watched for a driver to approach. G2 held out his thumb. "Headed West, old timer?" the driver asked. G2 nodded. "Well, there's no sexy blondes standing in the parking lot waiting go with me, so hop in. Piss now, though. I won't be stopping until Denver." G2 relieved himself next to the trailer rig and climbed up into the cab. "God bless," he said as he settled in. "He better," said the driver. "But just in case, you better buckle up, pardner. And no booze till we stop. Don't mind if you're quiet, I talk enough for both of us." The big rig lurched forward toward the freeway entrance and then began to whine as the driver shifted through the gears and the truck gained momentum. The freight train G2 had seen was soon in sight on the track that paralleled the freeway. As they came up alongside the train, G2 began counting the cars.

"I prefer this section in the daylight," the driver said after introducing himself to G2 as Jimmy. "Come across the plains in the dark. Stopped about three and got forty winks and a bucket of coffee. Now I can make it over the mountains in daylight and see if I'm about to go flying off a cliff. We're going to put the hammer down and take this rig to Vegas, baby." It was a long ways to Vegas, G2 thought absently. They were passing the cars of the train steadily and Jimmy swung into the passing lane to go around a car with kids pumping their hands up and down. Jimmy obliged with a quick toot on his air horn when he was up beside the car. The kids went wild and immediately went back to looking out the back window. They'd passed nearly a hundred cars of the train so far and Gerald thought he could see the engines ahead. "Good thing you found me, pardner. If you were on that train, you'd go into those tunnels west of Denver and wouldn't see the sky for an hour at a time. Oh we'll have some tunnels, too, but they don't send road traffic underground all that much. We'll get a good head of steam up before we hit the foothills and we'll be almost to Denver before we lose the inertia. That's what trucking is all about — inertia. It's easier to maintain a speed of 70 miles per hour up a mountain than it is to maintain a speed of 20 miles per hour. I intend to be doing 85 before the first pull starts." One hundred forty-two cars and four engines, G2 thought as they left the train behind. From the cars the train had been passing, G2 figured they were building up a head of steam, too. Only there weren't state troopers and stop lights when you were on the train.

◆◆◆

GERALD STARTED COUNTING CARS on freight trains when he was just learning to count. His parents were taking him on a road trip to visit a grandfather or an uncle somewhere in Southern California. His sister was just a baby and Gerald was impatient to be out of the car. And then they were stopped at a railroad crossing with a long freight train headed across. "Let's see if you can count all the cars," his mother cajoled him. And so they had all counted as the slow moving freight train crossed in front of them. Only 64 cars, Gerald thought. Then immediately skipped to complaining about how far it was to where they were going and when they would get there. "Gerald, if you keep complaining, I'll drive right past grandpa's house and keep driving all night long. You'll find out how big a country we live in. Gerald was sure it was big because he couldn't remember how long it had been since they left home. It was days and days ago and he was tired of traveling. His mother took a different tack. "Let's see who can find all the letters in the alphabet," she suggested. She explained that there were lots of letters alongside the road and on license plates of the cars they passed. "A, b," she said pointing to a sign that said "Bailey, 25 mi." "C," his father said pointing to a Colorado license plate as it went by on the left. "D," Gerald sang out as he pointed to a "Deer Crossing" sign. The family got stuck for a long time on "Q" until they all saw a billboard advertising "Antiques." It took many miles to get all the letters and Gerald spent much of it looking at license plates of cars that passed his family's much slower vehicle. His mother passed him a United States Road Atlas and Gerald started collecting license plates from each state in the union. When he saw a new plate, his mother would say "Indiana. The capitol of Indiana is Indianapolis." Then she would point out the state and the city on the map. It was not long before Gerald could find the states himself and name all the capitals. His mother spent much of the trip facing the back seat. Soon it became Gerald's game. "Idaho. The capital of Idaho is Boise. Idaho touches Washington, Oregon, Nevada, Utah, Wyoming, Montana, and Canada. The capital of Washington is Olympia. The capital of Oregon is Salem. The capital of Nevada is Carson City. The capital of Utah is Salt Lake City. The capital of Wyoming is Cheyenne. The capital of Montana is Helena." If his mother didn't stop him he would start with Montana and name all the states that touched it and their capitals and so on. Gerald was very good at geography. He knew all the states and their capitals.

◆◆◆

"WHEN I WAS A KID," Jimmy said as they pulled away from the rest stop outside Denver, "all I ever wanted to do was drive. I wanted a Dodge Charger like the General Lee. 425 cubic inch V8 Hemi 2x4. Wanted one that was gloss black, not orange like the General. I was just going to drive that dog from coast to coast. Take every U.S. Highway there was. U.S. 20. U.S. 6. Route 66. The Coast Highway in California. I was going to just drive until I ran out of road. Turns out I ran out of gas. Or money to pay for it. I couldn't afford to buy a Charger. But I loved to drive. So I figured driving is what I'd do for a living. Started off driving local deliveries. Then panel vans. Got a big break one day when a fella I knew decided to upgrade his rig and I got my first cab for a song. Course I say that now. When I bought it I had to mortgage my life. Thought I'd never get it paid for. But my buddy hooked me up with a guy who sold horse trailers down in Chickasha, Oklahoma. He had to have a batch delivered someplace nearly every week, and I was there to do the driving. First time I pulled out of the lot with a load of trailers on a big flatbed was the first time I pulled a trailer with that rig. It took me two days and two gallons of coffee to get those trailers to Illinois. Every time I looked in the mirror I expected to see a cop. I couldn't take my hands off the wheel to make a call on the CB. I was a real rube. Then I turned around and was about to head back when the guy I delivered to says, "You running empty southbound?" "Rather not," I said. "I got a load of hay that'll get you to Joplin," he says. I loaded up and took hay to Joplin then hooked up a cattle trailer and headed into St. Louis. They told me about some tools headed for Chicago, and from there I picked up a refrigerator trailer and headed to Georgia. It was six weeks before I ended up back home and my wife had had a baby. Almost like being in the army. I spent 287 nights on the road that year. We got a new Kenworth tractor with a bed over the back and took the wife and baby on the road with me. Almost seemed like we didn't need a house till she got pregnant again. Of course, she had to settle down with the kids while I hit the road and brought in the money to pay for the brats. We stayed together till the boys were out of school, then she decided she'd had enough of me being on the road all the time and moved back to Ohio. We still get together now and then when I get a run up to Akron, but I mostly just live in the tractor now."

G2 had counted 847 telephone poles since Denver.

GERALD HAD ALWAYS FOUND counting things to be comforting. It seemed he didn't have to worry if there was something to count. They'd received forty-seven Christmas cards one year. It was the first year that Gerald had an advent calendar. It was a card from Aunt Claudia. His mother set it up and each day in December Gerald opened a window on the card. Behind the window was a little picture of a treasure—candy canes, bicycles, wrapped presents, a doll. On the 25th of December he opened a door that showed a picture of Santa with his reindeer flying away wishing everyone "Merry Christmas." Gerald's favorite Christmas carol had been "The Twelve Days of Christmas." It was a counting song. There were often thirteen steps in a flight of stairs between two floors, but big buildings never had a thirteenth floor. There were always an odd number of urinals in a men's room. Numbered streets ran east and west and avenues ran north and south. It was 5,217 steps from home to school if Gerald took the most direct route. Once Gerald had counted how many breaths he took in an hour.

Gerald had been in an accident once while driving back to school from the holiday break. It was the first time that he and Brian traveled separately back to school. It was January 5th, the twelfth day of Christmas and it was late at night. Gerald was counting the mileposts along the Interstate. There was a large green sign every mile, but every tenth of a mile there was a reflective cap on the roadside reflectors. 47.2, 47.3, 47.4. Gerald hadn't been consciously counting the tenths; just the miles. He came up over a hill just at the speed limit of 70 miles per hour when he found himself suddenly on a glaze of black ice. Gerald suddenly realized that he had no control over his car and that he was going to die, just like his father did. The car slewed sideways and Gerald could see a bridge abutment ahead of him. But the car wheels caught in the snow at the edge of the road and veered sharply to the right, missing the abutment. The wheels on the right side of the car dug deeply into the snow and the car slowly rolled onto its right side. Gerald hung suspended from his seatbelt as the right window and side of the car was torn apart and the car finally came to a rest nearly a hundred yards off the road. Gerald was not dead.

He turned the car off, but couldn't get the key out of the ignition. Shaken but not injured, Gerald released his seatbelt and pushed the driver's side door open. He slipped out before the door slammed back shut. He wandered back to the highway where a semi was coming over the hill at a scarce crawl. Even at such a slow speed he slid as he came to a stop and let Gerald into the cab.

"You got lucky," the driver said. "I saw you fishtail before I got to the ice and got the rig slowed down and under control before I ended up the same way. Guess I've got you to thank for getting me slowed down," the driver said. He switched on his CB radio and the chatter was rapid. "Sounds like we've got State Troopers ahead with a really big accident. Eight cars. We'll crawl up there and you can connect with them." By the time they reached the scene of the accident three miles further on, the CB had been alive with the news that the highway was being closed and all traffic was being routed off at the last exit Gerald had passed. When he reached for his wallet to give to the State Patrol, he realized he didn't have it. His wallet had been lying on the seat beside him. It took most of the night to get the accident cleared and get a tow truck up to where Gerald's car — his father's big Impala — rested on its side. When the car was righted, Gerald's ID and wallet were plastered on the side of the car. The big car had done its job one last time and Gerald was uninjured, but the car would not be driven again. It was at mile 194.4.

♦♦♦

SOMETIME BEFORE LAS VEGAS, Jimmy got quiet. "We're coming to sin city, pardner. If you want out here, I'll stop at Henderson and let you off, but I won't stop any closer. I'm not a religious man," he said, "but Las Vegas is filled with temptations that will destroy your soul. You think everything is a bargain. Free food, free drinks, and all you have to do is sit at a nickel slot machine and pull the handle for an hour. But the hour stretches to four and a girl who is not free catches your eye, and you leave the next day without a penny left for gas, a hangover that splits your head, and sense of shame that turns your stomach to Jell-O. Do you want out?" G2 shook his head. "Good. Then let's listen to the radio and arm ourselves against the devil." Apparently Jimmy was prepared well in advance. The radio button he pushed was a 24-hour gospel station. A preacher droned on and on about the sins of the flesh and the inevitable wages they brought. But Jesus could give you strength.

Gerald was eleven when he accepted Christ. He was on a river boat in the Wisconsin Dells. His parents, grandparents, and sister had decided to vacation near to home this summer and enjoy the sites. They had visited "Witches Gulch," on the trip already—a windy chasm with a small bridge that crossed it. Marian had lost her sun hat in the swirling waters below the bridge and was distraught. Grandma had given her hat to the crying girl. They saw real Indians perform at the top of a balanced rock, including leaping across the chasm at the top. The "Mystery Spot" was a favorite of Gerald's. Inside the cabin, gravity was different and you stood on the walls. And then there were the water falls. Glorious, high and thundering. The boat could go no further up the river, but just as they were reversing directions, Gerald heard a screech and looking up in a dead tree saw an eagle spread its wings and dance at the edge of its nest. Everyone on the boat oooooed about the display and cameras clicked pictures. An older man sitting near where Gerald was standing at the railing said, "One of God's precious miracles isn't it?" Gerald was not sure, but it was certainly beautiful. "What's your name, son?" the man asked. "Gerald," he responded. "Are you a Christian, Gerald?" Well, Gerald had never thought about it much. His family sometimes went to church, especially on Christmas and Easter, so he supposed he was. But the man gently explained about Jesus being the Christ and offering to forgive the sins of anyone who accepted him into their life. All they had to do was confess and believe, and they would be forgiven.

It happened that Gerald was struggling with a bit of a guilty conscience. When they were in the Witches Gulch he'd been behind his sister who, being little, wasn't moving as fast as Gerald wanted to. In a pique, Gerald flipped his fingers at the back of her hat. He didn't mean to knock it off, just to knock it down over her eyes. But a random gust of wind from the gully picked up the hat and carried it off his sister's head and down into the roiling waters below. Chances are the wind would have taken her hat anyway. Everyone who wore a hat was clutching it. But Gerald knew he was responsible for the loss and he hadn't told anyone. If Jesus could forgive him, then it would all be okay. So Gerald followed the man's instructions, prayed the words that he was instructed to pray, and accepted Christ. The man then gave Gerald a strange instruction. "I'd like you to walk over to that woman in the pink sweater at the rail and tell her you've just accepted Christ," the man said. This was going to take a little more effort than Gerald had planned. Do you just walk up to a stranger and tell her that you accepted Christ? He wasn't sure, but thinking of the hat in the Witches Gulch, Gerald steeled himself to the task and approached the woman. When he told her he had just accepted Christ, she smiled at him and said that was wonderful. Then she said she had something for him and pulled a tiny New Testament from her purse. She said that this was the word of God and he should read it now that he was a Christian She also pulled out a pencil and inside the front cover wrote several scripture verses as she quoted them from memory. "Behold I stand at the door and knock; if any man hear my voice and open the door, I will come into to him, and will sup with him, and he with me." Revelation 3:20. "For God so loved the world, that he gave his only begotten Son, that whosoever believeth in him should not perish, but have everlasting life." John 3:16. She kept quoting and writing the references in the front of the tiny New Testament until there were seven references. "You should carry the Word of God in your heart, Gerald," she said. "The way to do that is to memorize it. Start with these seven verses, and then memorize as many as you can. You will always have a scripture to help you through the day, even if you don't have your Bible." Gerald committed to memorizing the verses and was so happy about what he had done that he marched straight up to his parents and said "I accepted Christ as my savior today, and I think I might have been responsible for Marian losing her hat." His parents were surprised, but only said, "Thank you for telling us, son. That's very brave of you." But Gerald's father knew what to do. When they got home, he began taking Gerald to church every Sunday. It was summer and hot, and Sunday morning Gerald was used to getting together with Brian and playing in the willow tree behind the house. They'd built a fort high in the branches where they could see over the whole neighborhood. The preacher talked for a long time, and even though Gerald saw other kids he knew in church, they all left before the sermon and went to "children's church" in the basement. When Gerald asked if he should go, his father said simply, "No. They haven't accepted Christ yet." So Gerald sat in the church service every Sunday morning. In two months, church had cured him of Christianity and he told his father he'd rather not go anymore. His father simply said all right, and the subject never came up again.

But Gerald had memorized the seven verses and when G2 heard the preacher on the radio say, "Study to show thyself approved unto God, a workman that needeth not to be ashamed, rightly dividing the word of truth," G2 mouthed the words, "Second Timothy 2:15."

WHEN G2 SAW THE LICENSE PLATE on the car parked at the curb, he immediately got his little notebook out and wrote down the num-ber—*letters*, he corrected himself. "BGOOD." It was very exciting. He was, after all, GGOOD. His sister would have been MGOOD. He wrote all the ideas down. He thought perhaps he should wait for the owner to come back to the car and introduce himself. They were prob-ably related. G2 tried to think who in his family had a name that start-ed with B. Carl, Wayne, and Harry were his father and his father's brothers. Their wives were Mary, Claudia, and Kim. They had chil-dren. Let's see. Meredith, Michael, Tracy, Susan, Dora, and of course Marian and Gerald. The only boy besides G2 was Michael, but G2 didn't know if Michael had any children. That would mean that the relative that owned the car was more distant than cousins, aunts, and uncles. What did they do in the state when they had more than one person who wanted the plate? Mary, Marian, Meredith, and Michael would all be MGOOD. MGOOD1, MGOOD2, MGOOD3, MGOOD4. Maybe they would issue them in birth order. By the time G2 had gone through all these possibilities, he had already wandered down the street out of sight from the car with the important license plate. He sat and put out his sign. It would be good if he could get enough money to get another bottle. He was sure to run out tonight.

◆◆◆

THERE HAD ONCE BEEN a time when Gerald fancied himself a connoisseur of wine. Of course, that only lasted a year. On his 21st birthday he walked into Shrum's Wine Shoppe, looking for something to celebrate his birthday with. He'd never had more than a sip or two of wine and knew nothing about wine or how to choose a bottle. He handled several, evaluating the design of the labels and comparing them with the price of the bottles. He discovered that a great looking label did not mean a particularly high-priced bottle of wine. But, he didn't know if that meant the flavor of the wine would not correlate with the price, or if some makers of low quality wines spent a lot on labels so their bottles would look more attractive. He held two bottles of wine in his hands, comparing them, puzzled over which would be suitable for his first legal purchase in a wine shop.

"Do you like a dry or a sweet wine?" a man said from just behind his left shoulder. Gerald was startled and almost dropped the bottle in his left hand. He turned to see a stocky man in a white shirt and red apron with the wine shop's logo on it. The nametag he wore said "Leo."

"I don't really know," Gerald said. "I've never actually drunk wine before. It's to celebrate my 21st birthday."

"Is that today?" Leo asked.

"Yes."

"Good. If it was tomorrow, I'd have to ask you to leave and come back Monday. But let's see if we can come up with the right thing for you." Leo carefully took the two bottles Gerald was holding from him and placed them back on the shelf. "It takes a pretty sophisticated pal-ette to appreciate this bottle. It's not the kind of thing you want to just sit down and drink without warning. And this one is so sticky sweet that you might as well just eat candy. Nice for dessert, but not a main course. Are you planning to serve the wine with dinner?"

"Yes," Gerald said. "My girlfriend is cooking and I said I'd bring a bottle of wine."

"What's she cooking?"

"Something Chinese, I think. She asked me if I like soo-flay." Ger-ald thought Leo choked for a moment, but the older man just cleared his throat and led him to a different aisle.

"Do you just want a wine for tonight, or do you want to learn about wines?" Leo asked.

"Well, I do want one for tonight, but I'd like to learn about wine, too. I think I will like wine. I certainly like the way it smells."

"Then let's set you up on a little program. I'll help you get a good bottle to go with your soufflé, but then we'll look at a couple more bottles that you can try on different nights. When you've finished them, come back, tell me what you think of them, and we'll choose a couple more. Keep a log book of your wines and what you like. We'll get narrowed down to wines you can enjoy on any occasion."

"I'm not rich," Gerald said quickly. "I can't afford more than $20."

"Not a problem," Leo said. "Since we don't know what you like, we don't want to risk wasting an expensive bottle. So we'll go with half bottles. They'll give you and your girlfriend each a nice glass and you won't feel like you've wasted a lot of money if you don't like one. Now, soufflé, you say." He led Gerald to an aisle marked French Wines and stopped. "We don't know precisely what your girlfriend is cooking in her soufflé, which, by the way, is an egg dish that puffs up in the middle. Don't slam the door when you walk in tonight or she'll be upset that the center collapsed. If she is serving something light in the soufflé, then go with this Pinot Gris. It's from the Alsace region in the northeast of France. You need to chill this wine. Refrigerating it is fine, but let it sit in your glass for ten minutes before you drink it. It's a spicy, rich wine like a German Gewurztraminer, but isn't as fat and lazy. It will complement spinach, white cheeses like Swiss or Jarlsberg, or seafood like crab. Now if she tells you she's using a strong cheese like Cheddar or Gouda, you should have a nice red wine. Let's try a Médoc, Médoc — a wine so good they named it twice. Actually, the region of Médoc is north of the City of Bordeaux on the Atlantic. But Appellation Médoc Controlee refers to only to a small area, also referred to as Haut Médoc. Now with this wine, you want to drink it at room temperature. But don't just open and pour it. You want to open it and let it sit on the counter for half an hour so it breathes. Pour less wine into the glasses, so you'll each have two glasses out of this small bottle." After Leo had selected the two bottles — just $15, much to Gerald's relief — he gave him lessons on how to drink the wine and what kind of words to write down in his journal. All the way through his senior year in college, Gerald went back each week for two or three half bottles of wine, keeping careful notes on the overtones and flavors, acidity, bouquet, and staying power.

G2 kept notes in his notebook after he volunteered. But they began to all look alike. Sweet, sour, acidic, fruity. The more G2 drank, the less those words meant. But he always kept Leo's instructions in mind, no matter what the wine was. Drink slowly. Hold the wine in your mouth. Feel it before you swallow it. Love it like your girlfriend.

◆◆◆

G2 CLIMBED UP the embankment in the center of the cloverleaf at the freeway entrance. It had been a long and profitable day. He got to the freeway exit while it was still dark and stood at the corner by the traffic light. People going to work in the morning were surprised to see a shadowy man standing at the intersection and the first few accelerated to get through before they were caught waiting with G2 beside them. But G2 walked up and down the exit ramp fifty feet, careful not to cross over to that part where he might be considered to be on the freeway. There was a "No Hitchhiking" sign on the entrance side just at that point. As G2 walked back up the side toward the intersection, a hand was thrust out a car window with a dollar bill in it. G2 hurried to the car to take the bill and whisper "God bless" just as the light turned and traffic moved forward. By the time the morning traffic tapered off, G2 had made $15. He walked two blocks to WinDixie and bought a sandwich, a bottle of water, and a bottle of wine. He spent an extra twenty-five cents on a pack of gum. If he got hungry later on, he would chew gum. G2 did not want to risk losing his spot for the afternoon commute. The afternoon commute was harder to work than the morning. People were in a hurry to go home. Instead of working the ramp, you work the feeder street where cars stop before turning onto the freeway. Once they had made the turn, nothing would stop them. It was also hard because the entry was on the passenger side of the cars instead of the driver's side. It was harder for people to roll down a window and hand out a buck when they were on the opposite side of the car. Still, he made seven dollars and that left him with ten dollars for the day after food and wine. But the only camp G2 knew of was three miles away at the next exit, so he resolved to spend the night right here at his good entrance ramp.

The county had piled dirt in the middle of the cloverleaf high enough to make a small hill. It was for noise abatement. They had even done some modest landscaping, but nothing that would require mowing. Just small trees and shrubs with kinnikinnick as a ground cover. He wished they'd chosen a different ground cover. Kinnikinnick was woody and poked in places uncomfortably, but G2 found a spot near the top of the mound, sheltered by trees where tall grass grew and he could spread his blanket in relative comfort. From his vantage atop the mound, he could see the airport a mile away with planes taking off and landing right over his head. He ate his sandwich and sipped just a little of his wine.

Gerald was no stranger to airports. The local airport when he was growing up was small and friendly. It encouraged people to visit and spend time watching the big planes on the runways. The airport had one of the best restaurants in town, at least in Gerald's experience. On Sunday, just before most people got out of church, Gerald and his family would drive out to the airport where they had reservations for lunch. It seems it was always on Mother's Day or Mom and Dad's anniversary. Once when Gerald was given the option of where he would like to go out on his birthday he had asked to go to the airport. Sunday brunch was a grand affair with a buffet that had every kind of good food that Gerald loved on it. He would make trip after trip to the food bar to sample different kinds of salads with mayonnaise and fruit in them, ribs, shrimp, and scalloped potatoes. His parents would have a glass of champagne when it was offered, mixed with orange juice.

But the best part was the airplanes. Every few minutes a plane would roar to life on the runway and lift into the air. "Have a good time in Chicago," his father would say. "Have a good time in Paris," his mother would respond. Eventually Gerald and his sister got to play as well. Have a good time in Texas. Have a good time in Boise. Just after a plane landed, the loudspeaker in the airport would click on. "American Airlines is happy to announce the arrival of flight 27 from New York City. Passengers may be met at gate 5. Because they always got to the airport before "the church crowd," Gerald's family was always seated right by the windows. They would sit and enjoy another slice of pie or cup of coffee long into the afternoon, after others had already eaten and left. Then Gerald's mother would say, "Let's go to the deck," and the family would troop to the observation deck on the roof. From there they could see all over the air field and back into town as well. The planes were much louder up here and Marian would cover her ears. They would walk around the base of "the tower," a raised observation deck in the center front of the roof. Once they were invited in to see the traffic controllers at work and Gerald discovered the relationship between the green dots on the screens and the planes that he could see in the air. It was amazing.

Gerald's favorite part was watching the people carrying luggage or rolling it on carts headed for one of the gates where they would march across the tarmac and board an airplane. Have fun in Timbuktu, they would say as they waved to the people getting on the plane. Sometimes people would wave back. Gerald would pretend they were relatives going to far-away places who would bring back exotic gifts from Japan. Sometimes he imagined they were soldiers marching away to war. Sometimes he would get a little confused and think one of the people was Gerald and that standing with his parents he had suddenly traded places with the man on the tarmac. But most of all, they were people with a purpose. They needed to get through the airport to meet someone or to catch a plane somewhere. And when they got to their mysterious destination, people would be waiting to greet them at the gate—like the young woman wrapping her arms around her husband's neck when he came through the gate, and kissing him urgently.

G2 had never actually flown on an airplane. But he still thought "Have fun in Paris" whenever one took off and flew over his bedroll on the top of the cloverleaf mound.

◆◆◆

G2 DIDN'T KNOW exactly where he was. Oh, he vaguely recalled the city he had been in, but he didn't seem to be there anymore. He vaguely remembered wandering toward the railroad yard, but he didn't quite know if he ever went there. He must have because he was certainly on a train now. G2 usually knew where or what direction the trains he jumped were headed. He would often see the names of towns he passed painted on the water towers or on the platform for passenger trains. But in spite of having been sitting for hours — days?? — in the well of the hopper car as it journeyed across the country, G2 could not remember where he had been or where he was headed. It wasn't an unpleasant feeling. G2 often didn't know exactly where he was. But this gave him a sustained impression of having lost all track of time and motion.

It had happened to him once in high school. Brian had introduced Gerald to his cousin, a very cute girl from a town about fifty miles away. Gloria and Gerald were instantly enamored of each other and began to date occasionally. Dating Gloria presented certain challenges. Gerald had to drive fifty miles to pick her up and do whatever they planned — usually a school event like a game and dance — and then when they ended their date and he dropped her off at home by midnight, he had to drive fifty miles home. Gloria was fun, but the drives were exhausting. One night, Gerald found himself driving the car down a country road in the early hours of the morning and suddenly had no idea where he was or how he had gotten there. He slowed the car, which was doing nearly 70, and watched carefully in the darkness for landmarks that would let him know where he was. Eventually he recognized a sign alongside the road pointing to the left. It said simply "Saw sharpening." Gerald breathed a sigh of relief. It wasn't the way he usually came home from Gloria's, but he knew where he was now and it was only about ten miles home. The trouble was, he couldn't remember anything after he kissed Gloria goodnight—that was some kiss—and walked back to his car. He looked at his watch and realized that had been nearly three hours ago. When he told Brian about the episode, his friend joked about Gerald having been abducted by aliens and having three hours of missing time. He even speculated that Gloria had sucked the soul out of Gerald and three hours later got indigestion and spit it back out. Gerald stopped seeing Gloria soon after that. He wasn't sure if it was just not right between them, if it was just too far to drive for a date, or if he wasn't sure if she hadn't sucked his soul from him and spit him out later.

♦♦♦

IT WAS EASY to see the scenery when you were riding in the open, barely sheltered by the slope of a hopper car from the rain that was splashing down. There was a puddle of water gathering in the corner of the well and G2 consciously ignored how far it was spreading by focusing out across the prairie. His sweatshirt had a hood and he drew it up around his face as he stared at the passing fields. It was funny. Not ten feet away from the train, you could see the individual raindrops almost suspended in air when you blinked. But the drops that fell nearer to the passing train were a blur and G2 couldn't focus on them. He'd often noticed the same effect when he looked at the ties under the rails. You could focus on a railroad tie as it approached you and hold your focus there as you closed the distance and turned your head to watch it recede behind you. But if you looked through the hole in the well of the car at the ties as they flashed by directly under you, you could never focus on them. They became a single constant blur that hypnotized you and took you into deep, deep sleep.

Everyone dreamed, G2 supposed, but some dreams were more real than others. Once in high school he had dreamt of a girl he had a crush on. He woke up suddenly from the dream, completely convinced that he had felt her breath on his cheek. He never dated that girl. Never even acknowledged the crush to himself. But he'd felt that breath and wondered if she had dreamed the same.

G2 dreamed of the eyes of a man. He was familiar. G2 had looked into those eyes when he was a young man and decided to give that homeless bum everything that he had and trade places with him. In the dream, they were friends and sat across a table from each other sharing a glass of wine and telling about their lives together. They had hamburgers and French fries like a couple of college buddies. Then there was a change in the rhythm of the rails — the speed that the train went over the joints. G2 became aware of the blur of the ties beneath the car and the encroaching puddle of water in the well that now ran out the opening.

♦♦♦

IN COLLEGE, Professor Anka explained about different modes of consciousness and the Hindu desire to reach Nirvana — a state of one-ness with the universe that left the mind free of the body. Gerald had even begun meditation, hoping to achieve that state. It had never quite occurred. But he dreamed.

One day Gerald was walking to class, absorbed in what he was doing. He turned left on Girard, not thinking that school was to the right. When he came to a pylon and a warning sign he came up short, not quite understanding for a moment why his path was blocked. He looked at the police officer standing nearby and asked, "Can't I get through here?"

"I don't really think you want to," the officer said. He pointed across the street and Gerald saw a huge crane swing a wrecking ball into the building on the corner. Bricks and glass came crashing to the street and sidewalk. It was just at the moment the ball struck the building that Gerald suddenly had a flash of everything that had just happened and realized he had dreamed it just two weeks ago. The barrier, the policeman, the specific words that were spoken, the ball striking the building, and the brick that tumbled from high up and rolled across the pavement to the sidewalk in front of him. Only the brick had not landed in the dream; it just kept flying. As Gerald watched, however, a brick was dragged out of the wall by the back-swing of the crane and came flying across the street to roll to a rest by the curb. The officer ducked a little, but quickly regained his compo-sure. "Looks like we need to move the line back a little," he called to a worker across the street.

"Officer," Gerald said, getting the attention of the man. "May I have that?"

"Want to have a closer look at your death?" the officer joked. "Be quick. We're going to move the barrier back up the street ten yards." Gerald grabbed the brick and took it with him the other direction toward school. He somehow thought the brick was proof of his story and he took it in to Professor Anka's office and set it on the desk. The professor looked at the brick and up at Gerald with a questioning expression. Gerald told the professor about the experience of the morning, about the dream, and how it was finished after he became aware of the experience of déjà vu. The professor nodded and explained how the mind was non-linear in its experience and it was completely possible that Gerald had been in a deep enough sleep that his subconscious was able to see into a particular possible future that happened to become reality. Then he held the brick in his hands.

"Tell me, Gerald. If the brick had not fallen after you realized you were experiencing something that you had dreamed, would it invalidate the rest of the experience? In other words, would you have written everything that happened up to the moment of the brick falling to have been a mere coincidence, but not a prophetic dream? That is what happens with most of our dreams. We see flashes of all kinds of things that might be, because the mind is firing different synapses when we sleep. Anything we dream might be, based on our experiences so far. Even the ridiculous monster attacking us, or standing naked in front of a classroom to teach, or suddenly realizing you have a final exam in a class that you didn't know you were taking and are totally unprepared for. Any dream is a 'could be.' But when all that happens is that you are startled by a strange shape, or teach a class that you are nervous about, or take a final that you are unprepared for, we don't see a close enough correlation to the dream for it to jar us. But it doesn't make the coincidence less real. The mind has seen a future, but not quite accurately for the one you experience."

◆◆◆

WHITEFISH, MONTANA. G2 was headed eastward and was through the mountains. G2 had not found Nirvana. He was merely blanking out another portion of his life. If he could do that with all his life, then what? Then would he never want a glass of wine again? Would he achieve oneness with the universe? Would he be happy? Satisfied?

Content? Nothing? The last seemed the most likely. G2 did not feel satisfied or content. Neither was he unhappy or depressed. He didn't feel anything. People might have said he was empty inside, but G2 wasn't empty. He wasn't a wine bottle. A wine bottle was worthless when it was empty. But it didn't have to be full to be worthwhile, either. A few drops was sometimes enough. No, G2 was not a wine bottle. Maybe he was a rock. There was a song about that when he was a kid, but G2 couldn't remember anything past the words I am a rock. But it couldn't be a rock like the one Mr. Barnes showed in science.

In sixth grade, Mr. Barnes taught everyone about geodes. Gerald had been fascinated during the part when Mr. Barnes taught about erosion. Everyone brought a stone in from their yards or driveways, and for one entire class period they sanded their rock. At the end of class, the rocks were put on display with labels that showed the differences in erosion for different kinds of rock. Gerald scrubbed at his rock with vigor through the entire class, but couldn't see any change in the size of his rock. It was just a little smoother on the one side on which he had worked. Paul's rock was almost gone he'd sanded so much off of it. And Sandra's had crumbled with hardly any sanding at all. Mr. Barnes said it was really a dirt clod and not a rock at all. Mr. Barnes knew everything there was to know about rocks. The day he brought a geode to class was one of the most amazing in Gerald's six years of school.

"Now what kind of rock is this?" Mr. Barnes asked the class. All the words they had learned to describe rocks bubbled out of the kids mouths. Igneous, sedimentary, marble, conglomerate, fossil. But Mr. Barnes said that this was a very special rock called a geode. He handed out plastic goggles to all the kids and they giggled at each other and how silly they looked or poked at each other's eyes with their fingers. But when Mr. Barnes put on safety goggles, nobody laughed. Then he pulled on heavy leather work gloves, and finally picked up a large hammer he called a mallet and a steel chisel. He marked out an area around where he worked and told everyone they had to stay behind the chalk line. Then he set the rock on the floor and placed the chisel on it and struck it with the mallet. It took only two blows of the hammer before the geode split open and revealed the crystalline formations inside. The class jumped from the flying shards of stone, but then everyone crowded in to see the remarkable inside of this unusual rock. For weeks after that demonstration, kids from class would collect large rocks and work diligently at trying to break them open with a hammer. Gerald never found a crystal geode. All his rocks were solid and if they split at all it was into thousands of tiny pieces, crushed by the hammer blow.

G2 wasn't a geode. He had no inside, so he felt nothing inside. He wasn't empty. He wasn't full. If the huge wrecking ball hit him directly, he would just crumble into sand and loose bricks and it would be no different.

◆◆◆

THE LICENSE PLATE said "READP21." G2 stared at it for a long time. Then it dawned on him. Read page 21. *Of what?* he wondered. It was obviously important. He shuffled up the street until he saw a newspaper discarded on a sidewalk table. He picked it up and quickly turned through the pages. There were only 18 pages. No page 21. It took G2 a few minutes before he could get his bearings and identify where the library was, but when he had decided he walked there with determination. He would check page 21 and find out what was so important for him to read. At the door, however, G2 hesitated. He recognized some of the men gathered outside the library. Some were local and one or two were transient. One of the transient men waved G2 over. Reluctantly, G2 approached the men. The guy who called him over was tapping a cigarette on his thumbnail to tamp it down more firmly. "You gotta light, G2? I gotta coffin nail needs a hammer." *Sam something,* G2 thought. He didn't know the man well. But it did happen that G2 had a match. He was saving it to light a campfire tonight, but he could spare one. As long as the wind didn't blow it out.

The matchbook read "Wabash College" on the front. On the inside it said "A Liberal Arts College for Men — Crawfordsville, IN." G2 wasn't exactly sure where Crawfordsville was. He didn't recall going through it, but maybe it wasn't far. There were only three matches in the cover. He pulled one out and offered to light the cigarette for Sam, but the man snatched the cover and pulled out a second match, lit it and puffed the cigarette to life. He offered the light to a second man with a cigarette, but the wind blew it out. He dropped the dead match and tore the last match out of the cover, lit it and managed to get the second cigarette lit before the match went out.

"College man are you, G2? Goin' to the library to work on your Master of Liberal Arts degree?" The men laughed. G2 grinned and nodded. The library. That's where he was going. Sam tossed the empty matchbook on the ground and G2 picked it up. There was something about it that he needed, though he didn't know what it was. It was important. He would find out on page 21, he was sure of that. "You go get educated and when you make a million bucks, come get us and make us foremen, you hear?" Sam said. The men turned away from G2 and passed the two cigarettes around their little circle. No one offered a puff to G2. That didn't matter, really, because G2 never smoked, but it would have been nice to have been asked. Cigarettes were bad for you. That Surgeon General made sure everyone knew it years ago. He published big pictures of people's diseased lungs and made the tobacco growers put danger labels on their packages. There was no skull and crossbones on a bottle of wine; that was for sure. It was cigarettes that killed.

G2 was still staring at the open matchbook cover when he entered the library. What book was the message in?

◆◆◆

WHEN GERALD WAS A SOPHOMORE in college, his Early American History professor and his English Composition and Creative Writing professor assigned a joint research project that would last the entire semester, culminating in a 20-page term paper that would count as one-third of the grade in each class. The professors would grade the papers separately, so it was possible to receive different grades in each class. The paper was to describe the Revolutionary War as a common person might have experienced it. The professors had a grab-bag of names and a one paragraph biography of each person. The subjects came from different parts of the colonies and England. None were historical personages, but were identifiable in genealogies, letters, or historical references. The objective was not to research that person, but to research what the experience of that person could have been, based on the available data about the events of the war, the location of the person, their status, and family. Historical data had to be factual, but the paper had to be written from the point of view of the subject.

It was a daunting task. His personage was Sibel Betts, wife of Selah Betts of Pawlett, Vermont. Gerald went to the library with a general plan of research, starting with the Betts surname and extending to the town of Pawlett, thence to the state of Vermont and battles of the revolution that were fought within the region. He would track troupe movements and see if he could find the records of surviving soldiers from that region. He knew that one resource would be the Daughters of the American Revolution. The DAR had played a role in Gerald's high school life, even though no one in his family was a member. Each year the DAR sponsored an essay contest for seniors, awarding a thousand dollar scholarship to the winner. Gerald's essay had been chosen as a finalist in the competition. The five finalists presented their papers at a meeting of the DAR. The members then voted on the readings and awarded the prize. Gerald's paper was filled with buzz words that he knew the ultra-patriotic organization would love. That was how he had been chosen as a finalist (the only boy among four girls). His presentation went well, his mellow voice filling the living room of Mrs. Hanes' house. His persuasiveness made the words, "In God we trust," and "conceived in liberty," ring true and moved more than one of the members to tears. He sat, confident that he would be awarded the prize. Then his classmate, Debbie, rose to give her presentation. They'd never got along that well, but her smoothness in including him in her condescending gaze as she began her presentation made him feel very small. "Madame President, Ladies of the DAR, and fellow competitors and guests. Thank you for this opportunity to present my paper titled 'The Role of Wives in the American Revolution.'" Gerald knew that he had lost the competition before she began reading. He had stood, said the title of his paper, and read. He did not salute the ladies or thank them. As he looked at the warm smiles around the room, he realized that he was a token. He was not a girl. He was not a Daughter (or Son) of the American Revolution. He had not followed proper etiquette. And he did not win. Debbie was voted the winner in a formality that even had the other female competitors grumbling.

Gerald went to the card catalog in the library just after the library opened and began researching. He compiled a list of specific books that mentioned his subjects, but after he had a page of possible references, he moved to the first section of the library in which he had found a book reference. The library was organized according to the Dewey Decimal system. He began in category 917 with a specific book, but the book next to it also looked interesting. He leafed through the pages, starting with the table of contents and then scanning the index. He looked for references to the names he had found, but discovered a reference to a Vermont Company under the charge of General Wolcott. This led Gerald to biography. Next to Wolcott's biography was Wallace. When the library announced that it would close in fifteen minutes, Gerald looked up realizing that he had been pulling books off the shelves and looking in their indexes for ten hours and had not stopped to eat. His notebook was filled with references and his back hurt from sitting on the floor between the shelves poring over the books. He had forgotten the subject of his paper.

♦♦♦

G2 ENTERED THE LIBRARY with determination. Wabash. W. Page 21. World Book Encyclopedia. W was in volume 21. Page 21, Volume 21. Read page 21. He pulled the reference book from the shelf and sat on the floor in the aisle to open the book in his lap.

The World Book Encyclopedia was a familiar reference. Gerald's father had bought the set from a traveling salesman and the books were delivered six weeks later in a big box. Also included in the box were a World Book Cyclo Teacher and the fifteen-volume set of Childcraft. The next year, they began receiving World Book Yearbooks. Gerald's family had an entire bookshelf dedicated to World Book. Gerald sat for hours leafing through the volumes, feeling like he had all the knowledge in the world at his fingertips. Learning games on the Cyclo Teacher taught Gerald about constellations and he could still sleep outside at night and name all the major constellations in the northern skies. There had been only 20 volumes in the family World Book Encyclopedia, but the set in the library had 21 volumes with WXYZ all in the last book.

WAAF, Women's Auxiliary Air Force in Britain in World War II.

Waag, a river in Slovakia.

Waalhaven, The Netherlands, a Dutch military air field in World War II.

G2 turned over several pages. WABAC, the machine that Mr. Peabody used on the Rocky and Bullwinkle Show. G2 giggled over the memory of the cartoon. He had spent hours watching the clowning squirrel and moose. He loved Boris and Natasha.

Wabakimi Provincial Park in Ontario.

Waban, Massachusetts. G2 was sure he was close. He turned to page 21. Wabar Craters in Saudi Arabia. Wabash, Indiana. Census information, geography, historical sites. Nothing stuck out to G2. It must be here. Why was he supposed to read page 21. Wabash, St. Louis & Pacific Railroad Company vs. Illinois 1886, also known as the Wabash Case. The courts had to decide whether the states had the right to regulate railroad rates for interstate shipments. This was important, G2 thought. If every state could regulate who could travel or how much it cost on a railroad, then he might not be able to go through some states. G2 couldn't think of a state that had prevented him from riding the boxcars. There were conductors who locked cars, chased away bums, and occasionally did a sweep to be sure no unauthorized people were riding the rails. But not the states. The commerce clause does not permit states to enact direct burdens on interstate commerce. There you had it. He could ride the rails. Wabash led to the creation of the modern regulatory agency and signaled the movement of the national government to assume responsibility for economic affairs. Yes, the United States government was responsible. The courts had decided. When was that? In 1886. The courts had decided that Illinois couldn't regulate the railroads. Maybe he should sue the state. There were hardly any boxcars left on the rails. States were making the trains carry containers, two long and two up. When those cars ran empty, they were open and exposed to the air. Cold. Enclosed boxes were much better. Best thing you could get now was the well beneath a hopper car. You wanted to be on the trailing end of the car, or the wind would whip you to shreds. G2 opened his notebook and carefully wrote beneath the license "READP21" the word "Wabash." This was important. He carefully reshelved the encyclopedia and walked out of the library with determination. The states were changing the railroads and Wabash said they couldn't do that. G2 had an obligation to defend the railroad. That was what his journey was about.

G2 fished in his pocket to see what kind of money he had and then went into a 7-Eleven store. He bought a bottle of wine and filled his water bottle in the restroom. He bought a loaf of bread, though it pained him to pay so much. He had just enough left for a jar of peanut butter. With his supplies in hand, he headed for the tracks. Eastbound. He stopped beside a car and watched the brakeman as he came up the tracks checking the couplings. When he got to where G2 was standing, G2 recognized the man.

"G2. How's my man? Headed South?" the brakeman asked. G2 shook his head and pointed East. "East, huh. Jump over two lines to the Capitol. She'll pull out around ten tonight. Get ya east as far as ya want ta go." G2 bobbed his head and said "God bless," and then ducked under the car to cross two tracks and walk the length of the train before he found an empty well-car. He climbed aboard and waited for the train to move.

◆◆◆

THERE WAS A TIME when train conductors were the enemy. They jealously guarded their empty freights and would physically abuse hobos who jumped their trains if they caught them. Some had been rumored to have murdered bums, though no evidence had ever come to light. But times changed. Some of the short lines had managed to eliminate conductors and the cabooses they lived in altogether. Now, if there were two people on the train, it was the engineer and the assistant engineer. It was unusual for a freight to even have an extra brakeman these days. The engineers had too much to take care of to worry about a guy hitching a ride on an empty car. If someone jumped off the train or fell between the tracks, chances are it wouldn't be known until the next train came by. Could be later in the day or later in the week. Now dropping between the cars onto the tracks when the train was going 80 miles per hour would be a messy way to die, G2 thought. And it would hurt. Jumping from a train, though — say a train that was traveling over Crooked River Gorge Bridge in Oregon, 300 feet over the river — would be like flying right until the moment you died. It would be instant.

Flying would be fun. G2 had never been in an airplane, but that wouldn't really be flying anyway. Now standing on top of a boxcar at 80 miles an hour with your arms outstretched to the wind was like flying. If your clothes were too bulky, you could really be flying. Sometimes when he was out in the middle of nowhere—especially at night—G2 crept up the ladder to the top of his car and imagined he was flying. There was nothing but the wind and the darkness. And risk. G2 had once narrowly missed having his head taken off as they went through an underpass. It was a change in the sound of the rails that alerted G2 to pull his head down. That was the thing about riding the rails. Old timers said the steel talks to you. You could feel the difference when you crossed a state line. You could feel the change of speed. The steel would tell you when you were coming into town, what the weather was, and who was on the train. You could really feel the steel.

G2 thought about flying sometimes. Dropping off that bridge and living his last moments flying through the air. But he couldn't see the point in suicide. He wasn't unhappy. He just thought too much and the thoughts filled his head till it overflowed and there wasn't any way to escape from them. There had been a time when he'd thought about suicide because he was never going to be any of the things he assumed he'd be, but if any of those things wanted him, they'd find a way to have him.

◆◆◆

THAT'S WHAT IT WAS LIKE with Sharon. It was fall of Sophomore Year in college. Before school started Gerald and Brian and half a dozen other men and women in their class had decided to go camping over Labor Day before they had to buckle down and study. The group had done everything together over the past year. They met as part of a team selected to decorate the homecoming float for the Freshman Class They ate meals together in the dorm kitchen with a different member of the group cooking once each month. They had nicknames for each other drawn from *Winnie-the-Pooh*. Who were Pooh, and Piglet, and Eeyore? Gerald was Owl. Gerald had never actually read *Winnie-the-Pooh*. The friends went to ball games together and became a team for the annual bicycle relay race. They were on the rope together for the freshman/sophomore tug of war. Most of them studied the same things through their freshman year. Some of them had already paired off. Those who had were sharing a tent with each other, but most were sleeping head to head near the fire. Gerald was head to head with Sharon. She was quiet and studious. A nursing student, so she didn't share as many classes with the rest of the group. Rachel had brought her along to the float building and she had become one of the Pooh Corners group by virtue of her presence. Most things happened that way, Gerald decided. You just went along and people accepted you in or excluded you. That was how you knew where you belonged. It had happened to him often enough. Brian had led him into the business program and Gerald figured that was as good a major to study as he could think of. He didn't know exactly how it began, but lying head to head, whispering in the dying firelight, Gerald found himself kissing Sharon. Kissing had led to petting while those around them slept, many having drunk themselves into a stupor. Kissing and petting was much better than drinking, Gerald thought. And they became more and more urgent in their explorations. Sharon was panting into his mouth when she whispered that she was coming up. Gerald realized that from her perspective, he was up and barely got his sleeping bag open enough for her to slip into it with him.

It was an old army surplus sleeping bag. It wasn't that Gerald couldn't have afforded a better or more modern sleeping bag, but he'd had this one for years and never thought about replacing it. Where other campers were cocooned in arctic bags, Gerald's was large and flat, really made for lying on a cot instead of on the ground in a campground by the river. As a result, though, Sharon was able to slide into his bag with ease, and Gerald noticed as she did that she had already shed her jeans in her own bag. Lying in the sleeping bag with their bodies pressed against each other, the kissing became more passionate. Piece by piece, they stripped away the rest of their clothing and Gerald realized that he was about to have sex for the first time in his life. "I don't want to get you pregnant," he whispered as Sharon stroked him. "I'm on the pill for medical reasons," Sharon said. "I've never done this, but I want to." The thought of pregnancy had entered Gerald's mind and consumed him so much he scarcely heard her say she was on the pill. His erection suffered. Sharon was diligent, however. She had decided that this was the time and Gerald was the boy. But every time they made contact and Gerald tried to enter her he began to wilt. He was embarrassed by his inability, and that made things even more difficult. At last, frustrated that she could not force Gerald into her far enough to let go of him, and limited in what they could do by the dimensions of the bag and effort to stay quiet so they wouldn't wake anyone else, Sharon simply rubbed his cock in her slit until, gasping in their kiss, she came. It seemed impossible to Gerald that his first time actually ready to make love to a woman, he was unable to perform. Sharon kissed him again and then slipped out of his sleeping bag and back into her own. Gerald appreciated the sight of her naked body in the moonlight as she turned to wiggle into her bag. They giggled slightly as Gerald dove repeatedly into his sleeping bag to retrieve articles of clothing, sorting out which was hers and which was his. In the course of this relaxed play, Gerald became hard — really hard. "Sharon, I think I'm ready now," he said. "Shhhh," she said. "Go to sleep." She tucked herself into her sleeping bag and was asleep — or seemed to be — before Gerald could say anything else. She had been in his sleeping bag. They had been naked together. His cock had been at the entrance of her womb. She had rubbed him in her own juices. He touched himself once and came.

He never got together with Sharon again. He had asked her out once that fall, but she said she was really having to study harder this year and wasn't going out. Sharon was the first of the group to slip away and find other friends. Robin and Dave were in a world of their own and seldom did anything with the group of friends that year. Phillip quit school halfway through the term and joined the army. Carol announced that she was marrying a guy she met in Chem Lab at Christmas and was hardly seen by any of the group, though they all went to the wedding. At last there were just Gerald and Brian, studying together, signing up for the same classes, double-dating when they could. Gerald met the transfer student, Lori, during spring term and they had seldom been apart the rest of their time in school. She had taught him how to be a good and patient lover and not to be concerned about his performance. He had never had a problem answering her call, no matter what he was doing or how he felt. It was just a natural fit, though Gerald couldn't remember having ever really decided to be sexually active with Lori. She decided when and where. That was the way it was supposed to be.

♦♦♦

THERE WERE TOO MANY thoughts in G2's head. He didn't think he missed Lori. He could hardly remember her—just that she had been important. He stood at the edge of the well car leaning out into the night, feeling like he was flying, and let himself go.

G2 hit the cold steel bed of the well car with a clang that nearly knocked him unconscious. "That was so cool!" Mad Mary said, putting down her video camera. Mad Max held the back of G2's jacket as he dragged him away from the open bottom of the car. "It was like you were flying and were just a lifting off like an angel. I want to try it." It wasn't likely that Mad Mary would succeed in lifting off anything. She outweighed G2 by several pounds and was a lot more compact. "I knew you wouldn't want to go without your bag, though man," Mad Max said, shoving G2's canvas bag toward him. "It would have made great video, though."

Mad Max and Mad Mary weren't really homeless. Not that they had a house in the suburbs or anything, but they were self-styled documentarians who traveled the rails video-taping the transient homeless as they moved from one place to another, and then uploading the videos from their laptop computer to someplace where people could see the pictures. G2 was lost as soon as they opened their computer, but they showed him the video of his near flight into the unknown.

"You might think we're strange, just traveling around the country like we do," Mad Max had said. "But it beats having a mortgage and 2.5 kids to take care of. We were just going to travel for six months after we graduated, but that's been almost two years ago now. We're big sellers on YouTube. When we're ready to quit this life and settle down, we've got job offers from two television news stations. They've been running a weekly spot on us for nine months that we let them air before we put up on YouTube. This is definitely going to be on the news next week in Albuquerque."

"We've always hoped to catch up with you, G2. You're a hobo legend." Mad Mary pointed to the scrawl on the inside of the well done with a broad-tip marker. "G2." G2 remembered the day he marked his first boxcar with chalk. That would be long gone by now, of course. Chalk washed off in the rain or with a hose if the workers happened to flush out a car. Some itinerant homeless marked the cars with spray paint and you could see tags of all kinds on any train you boarded. G2 only ever seemed to have a pencil, but he marked cars with his pencil. Younger hobos often went over his mark with a marker to make it permanent. Once, G2 had ridden the rails in a car that was splashed with asphalt. He discovered that he could use the tip of his pencil to lift the tar and use it to create a raised impression on the wall of the car. His mark was much simpler than some of the transients—just the letter and number. The inside of this car had a dozen tags scrawled or painted on its low wall. "Rail Rider," "Steelman," "Zodiak," "Laze," and most recently the sprayed red heart onto which Mad Max had penned "MMax+MMary." During the relatively quiet period while their train had been pulled to a siding to allow a northbound to pass, Max and Mary filmed their two minute special.

"This week, we've caught up with legendary hobo, G2," Mad Max said, looking into the camera that Mad Mary held steadily on him. "G2 has been riding the rails for about thirty years, but you won't get a lot of information about his adventures from him. So far as we know, the only words anyone has ever heard him say are 'God bless.' Where are you heading right now, G2?" Mary moved the camera over to point at G2. Confused for a moment, G2 simply pointed the direction the train was headed. "South," Mad Max continued as the camera pointed back at him. There are a lot of cities south of here and sometime along the line you might see G2 standing at a freeway entrance with this sign." Mad Max held G2's corrugated sign up. It said, "Anything helps. God bless. G2." "G2's needs are simple," Mad Max continued. "Just enough money to buy a sandwich and a bottle of wine that will last him two or three days. G2 isn't a drunk; he isn't mentally unstable; and he isn't a danger to society. He is merely one of the hundreds, maybe thousands of unhomed people in this country that you see every day and simply don't notice. G2," Mad Mary turned the camera back on him. "Do you ever want to settle down, move into a home in a nice climate and quit wandering?" G2 was puzzled by the question, and it showed on his face. "Home" didn't really mean anything to him anymore.

◆◆◆

AT ONE TIME Gerald had a home. But when he left for college, his mother had sold the house he grew up in and Marian finished high school living in an apartment. That certainly wasn't a home. As soon as Marian got out of school she got married and moved into a real house in Seattle. She didn't consider the apartment a home. Gerald lived in an apartment while he was in college, shared with Brian. But neither of them considered the apartment home. "Home," said an old adage, "is where the heart is." Well, Gerald's heart lived firmly in his chest. The home that most people talked about always seemed to Gerald to be where their stuff was. His friends were constantly running home to get their ball glove, to eat, to watch TV. The idea of home was meaningless, Gerald had once asserted in an essay in the college newspaper. "The idea of 'home' may actually be the root of all conflict. If you have a home, you have to protect it. Even nations war over boundaries in order to protect their homeland. The notion that a nation, a people, a culture, or a race might have a home means that they have something to fight for. Home is what is threatened by different ideologies. Home is what people establish to provide a safe environment to raise their children. But our increasingly transient population is laying waste to that concept of home. Where settlers once put down roots and children grew old and died in the same house that they were born in, today the world is shrinking and people move hundreds of miles simply to take on a new job or marry a lover. Perhaps one day the world will become so small that we will all consider it our home and join together to protect it rather than spend our lives fighting over it." It was a good, if controversial essay, Gerald thought. Of course, he would never actually give up his own home. When he and Lori were married, they would raise children in their home and those children, while they might occupy a different building, would always have a place to come home to.

◆◆◆

NOW THE CONCEPT of home seemed completely foreign to G2. His heart was in his chest where it belonged, and all his "stuff" was in the canvas bag he slung over his shoulder. That seemed to be all the home he ever needed. Some hundred miles down the track, Mad Max showed G2 the video that was cut together from what they had filmed. Mad Max narrated and Mary's video cut to scenes of G2 flying in the wind, his tag on the car, his puzzled look, his cardboard sign. Following the closing remark, the camera zoomed in on the heart tag of the pair and then cut back to G2 who was smiling and nodded to the camera as he said "God bless." The train pulled into Omaha and Mad Max and Mad Mary jumped out. "Gotta find a place to plug in and recharge the batteries," Mad Max said. "We'll find a WiFi hotspot and upload the video, too," Mad Mary said. "God bless you, G2." G2 kept on the train to Atchison, then jumped off and headed further south toward Kansas City. Maybe he'd go on down to Texas.

◆◆◆

TECHNICALLY, Nate wasn't a panhandler. He told folks that, including police who happened by. Nate was a street musician—an entertainer. He was often seen near the public market in one city or the city square in another. Nate was always careful to set up where people did not have to step around him to pass on the sidewalk, but had easy access to the small guitar case that he set out to collect donations. Technically, Nate told the police, he wasn't asking for money at all. He was simply performing for the joy of making people happy and some of them saw fit to tip him. He played on his ukulele and sometimes his harmonica—occasionally both at the same time. Sometimes he sang. Nate also told stories. Usually funny stories. Sometimes stories that he made up on the spot about a little boy or girl who happened by and in the story had a great adventure flying on a dragon or battling pirates on the open sea. Nate was a busker with a bicycle and traveled all around the country playing his ukulele or telling stories.

Some places in the country require licenses or permits for busking, but these are more often required for playing on private property, like a shopping mall, than in public parks, streets, or centers. A busker is more likely to be arrested or told to move along if he blocks a thoroughfare, is too loud, or aggressively solicits money. Nate was none of those, and so he got along pretty well with the police in most places. Since Nate had a bicycle, he was also likely to spend some of his hard-earned money on a room at the Y, but the pack on his bike included a small tent.

The other thing of interest that Nate's pack included was a coffee pot.

"I used to drink the finest espresso," Nate told G2 one night when they shared a campsite. Nate couldn't help but tell a story if he was able and G2 didn't interrupt. "A 4-shot Americano. Now that's real coffee. I couldn't go a morning without a cup of coffee, I tell you. I could drink a double-espresso right now and sleep like a baby all night long. It wouldn't bother me at all. I just like coffee. It's not like an addiction or anything. It doesn't really affect me. But a day is so empty without it. I know everyplace that serves free coffee. When you're out on the open road, you look for those rest stops where the local Kiwanis are serving coffee to keep drivers awake. If you are in town, you go to Trader Joe's or Cost Plus. They always have a sample pot of their best brew for people to try. If you're careful, you can get two or three of those tiny cups they serve without people getting mad at you. But times have been hard, G2. Sometimes you are just too far away from a free cup o' Joe. And that's why I have this." Nate reached into his pack and pulled out a coffeepot. It was dented and fire blackened, but G2 could still read the words marked on the side that said "Nate's Pot."

"The problem is that coffee's got expensive. Just can't go in and buy a pound of '8-O'Clock' anymore. But I got a deal. I went over to Whole Foods and they give away coffee grounds from the espresso machine. Every time they fill up the tray, they dump the grounds in a bag and give it to people for their gardens. I told them I've got a garden and would like some grounds. They give me this bag of coffee. So I just scoop up a bunch of the used coffee grounds and dump them in the pot, cover it with water and let it boil about ten minutes. You've got to let it sit for a while after you take it off the fire. Gives the grounds a chance to settle. You're still going to end up chewing your coffee, but won't be that bad. You pour the coffee off the top of the grounds and it's just as good as Starbuck's." Nate had been preparing a pot of coffee all through his story and offered G2 a taste. G2 didn't have a cup, but Nate let him sip out of his. The coffee was strong and bitter and left bits of grounds between G2's teeth. But, he guessed that if he were alone in the cold, a cup could warm you up after a cold night on the ground.

"My granddad loved coffee," Nate continued. "Lived up in the mountains in West Virginia and still had a wood stove that heated his house and on which he cooked all his meals right up till the '80s when he went to live in a home. I remember as a kid going to visit him and seeing a big old porcelain coffeepot on the stove. It was always there. Granddad would make himself a rasher of bacon and an egg for breakfast on that stove every morning. The eggshell would go right into the basket with the coffee grounds. That's where I learned you could reuse the coffee grounds. Granddad would add a scoop of fresh coffee on top of yesterday's coffee grounds and just set the pot on to perk away. When the preacher came over to visit, it was occasion for fresh grounds. Granddad would perk up a pot on the stove and then the preacher would fill his cup with hot water and put just a couple spoons of Granddad's coffee in the cup. Then they'd laugh about the preacher coffee and play gin rummy all afternoon."

Nate lapsed into silence as he sipped his brew. G2 took a tiny sip of wine from his bottle. Nate nodded his head. He understood.

◆◆◆

G2 SAT OUTSIDE the baseball stadium with his sign held in front of him. Sports crowds were good. He had walked through the parking lot on his way to his favorite entrance gate and inhaled all the delightful aromas coming from the grills on the backs of truck beds. Men and women were cooking hot dogs and chili. The coals were sizzling. The air was filled with excitement and laughter. People had come before noon for the 4:00 game and a few were already pretty drunk. As G2 passed a truck with a crowd of men and women, he couldn't help but turn toward the smells and grill. His step must have hesitated because in a moment he felt a hand on his arm. He turned, startled, to look into the face of a man whose eyes were bleary with drink. G2 was prepared to run as soon as the man loosened his grip, but the low gravelly voice, though slightly slurred, was not antagonistic.

"You eat today, man?" the man asked. G2 thought for a moment. No, that had been yesterday. He shook his head. "Dolores! Get me a plate with a dog and some tater salad and bring me a bottle!" There was a stirring on the bed of the truck and a redheaded woman moved to the tailgate to look down. "Who's your mommy, Buddy?" she asked to the entertainment of the group. "You are, darlin'!" he said. "Who's your little friend, then?" Dolores hollered back. Everyone looked at G2. "He followed me home. Can I keep him?" Buddy called back. "Only if you promise to clean up after him," Dolores responded and then passed a plate of food and a bottle of beer down off the truck to Buddy. Buddy handed the plate and bottle to G2. "Can't go to a ball game on an empty belly, feller," Buddy said, patting G2 on the back. "Tuck in." G2 didn't wait for a second invitation. He scooped up the hot dog and ate it in three bites. He swallowed a bit of beer to wash it down.

Beer was different than wine. Wine was meant to be savored. G2 always let the wine sit on his tongue, no matter how cheap or bad the wine was. It was drinking the wine that comforted him, not the result of being drunk. Wine was sometimes sweet and sometimes sour and some were so dry you needed a drink of water to wash them down. But beer was bitter by comparison. Beer was made to wash food down with. You drank it on a hot day to cool off, or after a bite of hot food to quell your tongue. Beers could go down one after another and never be noticed until you were passed out under a freeway overpass somewhere. G2 didn't bother to savor the beer or hold it on his tongue. He swallowed it after every bite and had an empty plate and an empty bottle in minutes. He looked up at Buddy with a smile on his face and said, "God bless." Everyone on and around the truck had been watching him eat in silence and let out a bit of a cheer. "I think he likes you, Buddy," Dolores called. "You run along now, old man," Buddy said taking the empties from G2 and patting him on the back again. G2 bobbed again and turned to hurry away. "Aw, weren't that nice," G2 heard someone say as he moved away. "Buddy's got a big heart."

G2 belched and realized that he didn't dare breathe on anyone while he was panhandling because unlike wine, beer left a telltale reek on his breath. G2 chose a submissive pose and sat against a light post about ten yards from the gate. He propped his sign against his knees and put his cup in front of him and lowered his head to his knees. This way no one would smell his breath and G2 could depend on the sign to give each passing stranger a good God bless. G2's position also enabled him to keep an eye on the cup. You had to watch for little kids, especially, though occasionally another bum would try to slip a bill out of your cup, too. Whenever G2 had a bill in his cup, he slipped a hand out and moved it into his pocket. People could look at a cup completely full of change and still figure you hadn't made anything, but two dollar bills in the cup and people stopped giving. Too many people thought bums on the street made more money panhandling than "honest people" made working their jobs. When the crowds had passed and the game had started, G2 stirred to gather his things together. He was stiff after sitting on the pavement for so long and he needed a bathroom or a convenient wall to piss against. A few feet in front of him, a ticket scalper was looking at the half a dozen tickets he hadn't been able to get rid of before the game. He looked around, but no one was waiting for a last minute bargain. "Fuck," he said softly. He walked over to G2 and stuffed a ticket in his cup. "Enjoy the game," he said as he walked off.

G2 didn't know much about baseball games and players these days. Occasionally some fellow would talk about the damn Raiders or something, but G2 wasn't sure if they were talking about baseball or some other sport. He hadn't been to a baseball game since he was a kid. But what he did know was that baseball stadiums had bathrooms and he could clean up a little without having to go to a shelter. So he packed his sign in his bag with his cup and took the ticket to the gatekeeper. The ticket taker looked at the ticket and at G2 and squinted regarding what to do. She called another ticket taker over to her. "He can't have a legit ticket, can he?" she asked. "Why not?" her companion responded. "Scan it and see." She pointed a device at the stub of the ticket and her machine beeped. "See?" said the other ticket taker. "Nothing wrong with his ticket. "But he's a..." she started. "He's a bum," the other responded. "But look at him. He's an American bum. Baseball's an American sport. Any American with a ticket has the right to see a game." He waved G2 through the gate. "Second tier, 211 Section." G2 headed for the stairs.

◆◆◆

GERALD WON A TRIP to see the White Sox play ball in Chicago by delivering newspapers. It was a big deal. Jason, the distribution manager, had a van and loaded eight carriers in the back of it and he and his wife drove them to Chicago early in the morning. They barely made the first pitch at 1:15 after the drive and finding parking. They were great seats for boys, as high up in the stadium as they could get and right over the top of one of the entrances to the lower tier, so there was no one in front of them. Ted Wills was pitching and Bill Skowron whacked a homer in the third. The game was exciting, but by the 7th inning, it was just another long sit. Gerald and his friend Salvador went out to buy popcorn while everyone else was singing "Take me out to the ballgame." They'd already had way too much to eat, but the popcorn gave them an excuse to get up and leave their seats. When they got back to their seats, Sal had the brilliant idea that they should see if they could toss a piece of popcorn into a guy's beer on the next level down. The boys got into this game more than the baseball game, laughing as each kernel of popcorn flew through the air and landed on a different person. They were suddenly startled by the appearance of a face directly in front of them. A cop was standing on a ladder in the entrance below them staring right into their eyes. "You think people come to a ball game to get popcorn thrown at them?" the cop snarled. "No sir," Sal said. "We're sorry, sir." "Give!" the cop commanded, holding out his hand. The boys handed him their bags of popcorn. "Now sit there and watch the rest of the game quietly or I'll throw you out of here." "Yes sir," both boys answered. They sat back in their seats without moving for the last inning and a half of the game. Gerald couldn't remember who won.

◆◆◆

THERE WERE CERTAIN CAMPS that were always risky to stay in, but sometimes the risks of staying on the streets alone were worse. Police downtown were on a rampage to clear the business district of people sleeping in doorways and on park benches. They were arresting people for vagrancy. That meant that after a speedy trial in the morning, if the bum couldn't come up with the money for a sizable fine, he'd be sent to a labor camp for 30 days. G2 had been in a labor camp once. They were sent out to pick up garbage along an Interstate highway every day. Sundays they were forced to stay in their dorms all day, but the county didn't count Sundays as part of the 30 days. Once every two hours, a truck would drive up the berm of the road and collect the black garbage bags the laborers left by the side of the road. They would offer a ladle of water to each laborer as they went. If you missed your water, you had nothing to drink for another two hours. They brought you a peanut butter sandwich at lunchtime, but you didn't get a break to eat it. You had to keep working. At night, after ten hours or more of picking up garbage, you were picked up in the same truck as the garbage and driven back to the dorm. There you got a bowl of watery soup and some bread and had to stay in your bed the rest of the night. G2 watched carefully all through the first week, but found no opportunity to escape. Thursday the next week, he saw his opportunity and just after the water truck had come and the guard's attention was focused on the next man up the road, G2 slipped over the berm of the track they were working next to. He could see the freight train approaching, just picking up speed as it left town. When it pulled up next to him, G2 ran beside it and caught hold of a side ladder. It almost jerked his arm out of his shoulder, but G2 hung on and quickly dropped down out of sight between two tank cars. He pulled off the yellow striped vest they wore along the road—bumblebee jackets, they guys called them—and the county issued coveralls. He stuffed the vest into the crack between the tank and the bed of the car. The coveralls he turned inside out and put them back on so people couldn't see the "property of county jail" stenciled on the back. The problem with escaping instead of serving out your term was that you had to leave with nothing. If you served out your thirty days, they paid you $30 and gave you your "personal effects" as they called them. If you skipped, they didn't come looking for you. You just didn't have anything when you left. G2 had been with nothing before. It didn't mean that much to be with nothing again. But he didn't ever want to get caught and sent to a labor camp again.

◆◆◆

IT WAS DIFFERENT with the labor whores. Cops left them alone and the ladies aid society at the church brought them coffee where they stood on the street outside the Home Depot. They gathered there every morning, but especially on Saturday and Sunday. Most of them weren't homeless. They were just unemployed or on strike or laid-off. They'd stand out there in their sturdy Red Wing work boots and leather gloves, posing like they were ready to lift a heavy object. Even in cold weather, some of the labor whores would wear T-shirts with the sleeves ripped off to show off their muscles. The women who sold their bodies near the theater district were often told by police to move on, their johns were arrested, or they were coerced into having sex for protection or to keep from going to jail. But no one bothered the men who sold their bodies. Every so often a guy with a truckload of lumber would pull up in front of the group standing on the sidewalk. He'd roll down his window and say, "Two guys, two hours, fifty bucks. Heavy lifting." Those who were willing to take the contract would step forward and he'd point to two and say "You and you. Get in the back." They'd hop in the back and he'd drive off. They would get to a construction site where they unloaded the truck, helped lift a stud wall into place. Load the truck with scrap for the dump, go with it to the dump and unload it, then be dropped off back at Home Depot with $25 each in their pockets. They'd nod at the others who were still their trying to sell their bodies and get in their cars and drive away. $25 might get them milk for the baby, or keep their wives from selling themselves in the theater district.

◆◆◆

G2 SAT AT A SMALL FIRE and took a careful sip from his bottle. Jess the Mess sat across from him. "We gotta get outta here," Jess said. "They chase us out of downtown. They keep us from sleeping in doorways. You think they won't chase us out from under the railroad bridge? Only reason they haven't been here yet is because they'd get their shoes muddy. They're gonna come." Jess had a good scheme going. He panhandled with a sense of humor. There was a small cut on his forehead that he opened every morning with his pocket knife — just enough to have a little fresh blood dried around what was a pretty serious-looking scar. Jess was a verbal panhandler and didn't have a sign. He'd just call out to folks who passed by. "I need money for an operation," he'd call. "Can you help a guy who needs an operation?" Inevitably someone would stop and ask what kind of an operation he needed. "I need a brain transplant. Look here," he'd say as he pointed to the scar and fresh blood. "They already took out the old one, but I don't have the money to put the new one in." People would usually laugh, but they'd also usually give the guy a buck for the entertainment. Problem was you couldn't stay in the same place with that kind of line because in a day everyone had heard it and you had to find a new place or a new pitch. Jess usually moved on. Tonight, Jess seemed more agitated than usual. "I'm not going back to the workhouse, I'll tell you that. Bitches want free labor to clean the chicken farms. Not going back there. I'll fight them first." With that Jess pulled a gun out of his pocket and showed it around. G2 started edging away from the fire.

◆◆◆

GERALD'S MOTHER AND FATHER were radical non-violence people. From the time Gerald could remember, no guns were ever allowed in his home. His father had served alternate service during the Korean Conflict, having refused to touch a gun. He never spoke of that time, but Gerald understood that he'd served as an orderly in a tuberculosis sanitarium. Of course Gerald had watched *The Lone Ranger* on television and wanted desperately to have a six shooter with silver bullets and a white horse. His father said, "No guns is no guns. No real guns. No toy guns." Kids being kids, when Gerald got together with his friends in the neighborhood in the summer, they played cowboys and they played army. Some of the kids had toy guns, but Gerald made do with any handily shaped stick as his weapon. The kids would run up the street dodging between parked cars and popping up to yell, "Pow, pow. Got you Jeff!" At which time Jeff would enact his death scene in the street and be out of play until one of his team could tag him and bring him back to life. The games, while simulating violence, were innocent and no one actually got shot or died or was hurt.

Not until Gerald was in high school. Jeff disappeared from the neighborhood that summer. He'd begun running with a pretty tough bunch of kids who were always looking for trouble. One night after basketball practice, Gerald was getting a ride home with Jan and Ron. On the street outside the school a carload of toughs pulled up beside them. Ron dove for cover in the bushes, but Jan turned to face the toughs as two piled out of the car. Gerald never really heard the conflict, but he saw Jan hit in the mouth and start to bleed. Gerald stooped slightly to drop his book bag and go help his friend. Just as he moved, the boot of the other tough grazed his head as the kid jumped for him. Assuming Gerald was down, both toughs jumped back in the car and it sped off. As Gerald watched them getting in the front seat, he saw Jeff in the back seat lean forward. Jeff pointed his index finger at Gerald and pulled it back like he was pulling a trigger.

"You owe me for the dentist!" Jan shouted at the car as it pulled away. He was still bleeding, but refused to let Gerald drive his car. He dropped Gerald and Ron off a block away from their homes and continued driving.

Jan was out of school for a few days and his face was black and blue when he returned. The dentist had managed to straighten and wire his teeth in place, so he didn't lose them, but he didn't eat meat for two months afterward. They never talked about the event. The one time Gerald brought it up Jan cut him off and said not to mention it. Maybe Jan thought Gerald wasn't going to help him. After all, Gerald was hardly touched. The kick to his head had all but missed him. Gerald wondered about that. Why didn't they hit him, too? It was easy to see why they would ignore Ron. He was half their size and hiding in the bushes, but both Gerald and Jan were fully standing on the sidewalk. Why the missed kick and nothing else? They had identified four of the six boys in the car, but of course the police just sent a warning over to the boys' homes and nothing was ever really done about it. They wrote it off to an interschool rivalry that got a little out of hand. Gerald came to believe that he was protected, maybe even charmed. There were bad things that happened around him every day. Not as bad as having a friend get beat up, but bad things. An accident occurred just after he'd passed the intersection. His car spun out on ice, but came to a stop facing the right direction and he was able to continue. Another car on the same patch of ice crashed into two parked cars and the driver was put in the hospital. But bad things didn't happen to Gerald. He thought that maybe his father had used up Gerald's quota of bad things when he was killed in the auto accident when

Gerald was almost thirteen. Maybe Gerald's father was still "always there" when Gerald needed him.

◆◆◆

JESS PUT AWAY HIS GUN and the guys at the fire kept talking but G2 kept moving further and further away until he was up next to the tracks on the trestle. He piled some leaves around him and huddled in his blanket. *First train that comes*, he thought. It was past the middle of the night when hell broke loose. Most of the action was on the other side of the tracks and trestle from where G2 huddled. There was no place further for him to go. He didn't like to walk across trestle bridges — especially at night. If a train came there was no place to get to safety. G2 knew stories of people who'd been caught unawares and were killed by an oncoming locomotive. Most of them were amateurs or drunk, but G2 was careful around bridges like that. They were dangerous. It's not that G2 never took risks. He'd once jumped from an overpass onto a passing train below him. He would probably have rolled off the top and been killed if one foot hadn't broken through the top of the cattle car he landed on and held him there. It happened that the car was full, so if he'd fallen all the way through he'd just as likely have been trampled to death. G2 pried the splintered wood away from his leg and crawled along the top of the cars until he found an open grain car. He sat in the grain and picked splinters out of his leg for the next twenty miles. But G2 remembered an absolute positive feeling that he would be safe if he jumped that train. He hadn't even considered what would happen if he fell off or fell through. He just acted. It was what he was supposed to do. And it was probably the right thing to do since he was being chased by a group of punks who had been going around town beating up homeless men. They didn't seem to need a reason, and as long as they weren't bothering regular people, the police seemed to be slow to act. G2 certainly wasn't going to wait to see if the cops would protect him.

G2 didn't feel safe when the police arrived under the trestle that night, either. There were dogs and lots of lights. Orders were shouted over a bullhorn down below as the police swept the area with powerful flashlights. G2 could hear Jess's voice booming out, "Hell no, we won't go!" Things were going to get ugly. G2 looked down the track to see redemption coming. The light of a slow-moving freight was coming around the curve to face the trestle. He crouched next to the track, ready to make his jump for the first available car. Then there was a gun shot from below and G2 felt panic take hold of him. The train was nearly there, but as G2 looked down the slope toward the water, he saw a figure come out from under the bridge, momentarily in the light, then in shadow again. There was a return volley of gunfire, then silence. Against the reflected light on the water below, G2 could see Jess moving up the slope. It was a steep ascent, G2 knew from having climbed it earlier in the night. Jess slipped and went down just as three police officers came out from under the bridge and began scanning the slope above them. With Jess down, G2 was the only thing visible above the police and as the light picked him out in the darkness, G2 leaped for the train. He felt the searing pain in his left leg and then heard the retort of the rifle below him. He hung onto the ladder as the train carried him out over the water on the trestle. The beam was swinging to pick him out again when Jess stood and started firing at the lights below him. There was an answering volley from below and this time G2 saw Jess pitch forward and down the slope toward the police officers. G2 dragged himself into the back well of a jimmie hopper car, but the lights did not return to scan the freight. They were focused on two bodies that lay at the bottom of the slope. It appeared that Jess would never get that brain transplant.

◆◆◆

G2 EXAMINED HIS WOUND the best he could in the darkness of the freight as it picked up speed. He wondered if there were still county hospitals where they took people to die when no friends showed up to claim them. But in spite of the pain and through the tears that ran down G2's cheeks, he knew he wasn't going to go to any hospital. The bullet entered the back outside of his left thigh and exited the back inside of his thigh. It looked like he'd had a spike driven through his leg, but it hadn't hit the bone. G2 opened his wine bottle and poured the last few drops into each of the wounds. He wept more — whether from the pain of the alcohol touching the fresh wound or from the loss of his last precious drops of wine, he was unsure. He pitched the bottle off the train and huddled in the corner of the well shuddering and crying. The salty tears ran through his beard and into his mouth. G2 slept with the taste of salt water on his lips.

◆◆◆

GERALD LOVED SALT WATER TAFFY. There was something special about the sweet saltiness of the sticky candy, especially if you got it at the county fair. It was even more exciting at this year's fair because he had a championship photography exhibit. All Gerald's friends were in 4-H, so it seemed natural for him to be in 4-H as well. Of course, he couldn't enter any of the animal husbandry categories. His family didn't live on a farm. They lived in the suburbs. They didn't even let him keep rabbits like Brian did that year. But for some reason, his mother thought he needed something to keep him busy this summer, so she entered him in three different projects in the 4-H Club. Head, heart, hands, and health, his mother said. It was a mantra that Gerald memorized since they repeated it at every 4-H meeting. The meetings were held at the local junior high school and it was fun. Gerald especially liked Woodcraft I. Each boy was given a piece of maple and a picture of a pig. Mr. Graves showed the boys how to use the flat of a pencil to cover the back of the picture with graphite. The boys taped the picture to the maple with the graphite down and carefully drew over the pig outline. When they untaped the pattern and lifted it from the wood, the drawing had been transferred to the maple. Each boy was given a coping saw, and over the next three club meetings, they cut the pig shape out of the wood. Then they were given sandpaper. "A cutting board," Mr. Graves told the boys, "needs to be smooth as glass so your mother doesn't get a splinter when she uses it." After they had smoothed the board, they oiled it with tung oil. That "raised the grain" and they had to use fine steel wool to smooth it back down to its glassy finish. Finally, the boys had to mark the spot for the center of the half-inch hole that would be drilled in the pig's tail so it could be hung on a peg. Each boy took his pig to Mr. Graves and positioned it on the drill press. Mr. Graves would pull the handle down so the point of the drill was just above the spot marked and ask if that was the right spot. The boy could adjust the pig until it was perfect and then Mr. Graves turned on the drill and bored a hole through the pig. Gerald's hole was off-center. In fact, it was so far off-center that there was scarcely any wood between the hole and the edge of the wood. Nonetheless, Gerald finished the project, sanded it, and entered it in the competition. He received a white participation ribbon for his efforts. His mother, who loved her new cutting board, often pointed out that some of the projects weren't identifiable as pigs at all and she didn't have a peg to hang hers from anyway, so the off-center hole didn't make a bit of difference. She loved it. She was still using it that last time Gerald had visited her.

But Gerald's presence at the Brown County Fair was not for his woodworking project, nor for the carefully collected and pressed leaves glued to a piece of poster board for his Forestry I project. Gerald was at the fair because of his photography project. Gerald's camera was not the greatest. He had a Kodak Instamatic 104 with a flash cube. Photography I was a competition for black and white photos. Gerald shot three 12-exposure cartridges of photos over the course of the summer. None of the shots were great. They were all in focus, though, and Gerald had chosen good subjects and composition. When they got the film and negatives back from Walgreen's Gerald had a hard time choosing which of the shots he should exhibit, so he took them to Indian Guides and showed everyone his photography. Something about the picture of two horses with their heads over the fence got Mr. Buckley to thinking. He spoke to Gerald's dad and the next day Gerald and his father took Gerald's negatives to Mr. Buckley. They talked about the project and about the rules for the entries. Then Mr. Buckley and Gerald's dad went to the dark room while Gerald and Dennis went out to play. Mr. Buckley had a good eye for composition and saw right away that Gerald had good subject matter that was hampered by the quality of the camera and the processing of the prints. He chose twelve photos for Gerald to exhibit and made new prints, improving contrast and using paper that would yield more solid blacks. When he saw the results, Gerald was very proud of his accomplishments. He carefully mounted the photos on his poster board, labeled them, and submitted his entry. Gerald's photo exhibit was the county champion Photography I exhibit.

And that was why Gerald was dropped off at the fairgrounds by his father on the way to work that Monday morning. The 4-H champions were photographed and interviewed for the local newspaper. Tuesday morning a two-page spread ran in the paper about the county fair and the exhibits that people would see when they went out to the DePere Fairgrounds that week. The problem was that the interviews and photos were done at 10:00 in the morning and nothing else at the fair really opened until afternoon. Gerald wandered through the horse barns, the cattle barns, and the sheep barns. He looked at the commercial exhibits, but they were all draped with sheets until the exhibitors and shillers could get there. He wandered the midway, but there was nothing open. No rides would run until 3:00 in the afternoon. That was when Gerald saw the big taffy pulling machine at work. The front of the Salt Water Taffy stand still had the shade pulled down, but when Gerald walked through behind the trailers, he saw that the door of the taffy wagon was open. He stood there rapt as the arms of the machine went around in opposite directions pulling the taffy first one way and then another. Two old people with white hair tended the machine and kneaded and rolled the taffy on the big stone slab then cut it into rounds. Gerald couldn't believe how fast their hands went as they wrapped candy and tossed the wrapped treasures into bins by flavor. As the man was taking a batch of candy off the puller, he caught sight of Gerald watching through the open door.

"Martha, we've got a spectator," he said. The woman turned from her work without slowing down as she wrapped and twisted the ends of the papers on the candy.

"Do you think it's an elf?" she asked. The man bent over to look at Gerald, then turned and flipped the mass of candy onto the kneading board.

"No, I don't think so. His ears aren't pointy."

"Now George, you know that the Northern elves have round ears." Then Martha paused and looked into Gerald's shining eyes. "But you are right. The pupils are round. Elves have vertical pupils, like a cat. What do you suppose it could be?"

"You don't suppose it's a child, do you?" George asked as he poured a ladle of fruit over the candy on the table and began to roll it up.

"A child?" Martha asked. "Whatever would a child be doing here? Why I haven't seen a child in twenty years." Martha stooped again, looking at Gerald and then asked, "Are you a child?"

"I'm a boy," Gerald said, almost laughing out loud.

"A boy? George, it says it's a boy."

"You don't say! Well, there's only one way to find out for sure." George came to the door. "You say you're a boy? Do you like salt wa-ter taffy?" Gerald didn't know. He told the man that he didn't think he'd ever had salt water taffy. "Well, let's find out," George said. With that he turned with a rolled piece of candy. "Now you have to take the paper off of this, and then you eat it. Not the paper — what's inside it. Can you do that?" Gerald nodded his head. He took the piece of candy from the old man, unwrapped it and popped it in his mouth. The first chew almost welded his jaw shut, but the burst of flavors was overwhelming. It was sweet with just a little hint of salt — and pepper-mint. It was delicious. Gerald loved it. This was the best thing he had ever tasted. "Do you like it?" George asked him.

"Yesh," Gerald said, his mouth was watering around the candy so much that he couldn't speak without slurring the word.

"It's a boy," George said proudly. "And just in time, too," he add-ed. "Do you have anywhere you are supposed to be?"

"Not until 1:00," Gerald said.

"Well we could certainly use your help, since you are a boy and all. It's slow work, but if you like salt water taffy, you could be our tester this morning."

"What does your tester do?" Gerald asked excitedly.

"Well, each time a batch of candy comes off the puller and we add flavor to it and start cutting the pieces, the tester has to take the first piece off the roll and chew it up to tell us if the batch is okay. Are you willing to try?"

"Oh yes," Gerald answered. Over the rest of the morning, Ger-ald had a piece of salt water taffy about every fifteen minutes as the couple expertly flipped each batch off the puller and put a new one on. The cut fruit, vanilla, cinnamon, wintergreen, jelly candies, and chocolate into the still hot candy as they kneaded it, rolled it, and cut the first piece off the roll to hand to Gerald. He pronounced every batch the best he'd ever tasted. During the course of the morning, they talked about his winning project and George and Martha both prom-ised they would go look at his pictures when the exhibits opened.

From that day on, Gerald had a weakness for salt water taffy.

G2 couldn't remember the last time he'd had a piece of salt water taffy, and that only made the tears run more.

◆◆◆

G2 WAS ON THE WRONG SIDE of the lake. It was the hottest summer he could remember and he had been heading west from New York. He got as far as Detroit and realized he would have to go into Chicago, or try to find a way around the northern end of the lake. G2 would have liked to go around the north, but the rail lines that went up that way had been abandoned long ago, which meant he'd have to hitchhike and take his chances. It was a bad territory to be abandoned in. But if he went south, he would have to go through Chicago and head north, a prospect that he also didn't relish.

◆◆◆

GERALD WAS THIRTEEN when Brian's father took the boys to St. Ignace, Michigan. In his own kind way, Howard was trying to step in to fill the void left by the death of Gerald's dad. On Labor Day weekend that year, they'd gone up to St. Ignace and walked the five miles across the Mackinac Bridge to Mackinaw City. Then they caught a bus back to St. Ignace. Gerald wasn't sure how to act on the trip. It had always been so natural when the boys went up with Gerald's dad. Even though Gerald respected Howard and even admired him because he worked in a factory, it seemed different somehow. But Howard was undaunted. He took the boys to the Mystery Spot, and Gerald was impressed that it was even cooler than the one he'd seen in the Ozarks. A ball actually rolled uphill. "Amazing," Brian said, when they got in the car. "Incredible," Gerald added. "You won't believe your eyes!" Howard chimed in. They all laughed and started using the words from the signs for the Mystery Spot for everything that happened. "How was lunch, boys?" Howard would ask. "Amazing!" Gerald said. "Incredible!" Brian added. "Mind-boggling," Howard said. He took the boys to the ferry terminal in St. Ignace and they boarded the boat to Mackinac Island. The Island was only reachable by ferry and Howard said that when they were offered the option of being included in the early plans for the bridge, the people turned it down emphatically. There were no cars on Mackinac Island and they wanted to keep it that way. They explored the shops and even went on a short horse ride. The horses proved to be so set on getting back to the barn, though, that they ignored the commands of the three novice riders entirely after about half an hour and took the shortest route back to the stable, crashing through underbrush and trying to lose their riders all the way. "Amazing," Howard said when they dismounted. The boys broke out laughing so hard they couldn't finish the lines. The trip back across the strait was harrowing, though. The winds had picked up and the passenger ferry was tossed around. Brian and his father stayed below, but Gerald felt compelled to be at the prow of the boat, as far out as passengers were allowed to go. He leaned out into the wind as the boat cut through the choppy waters, splashing a spray over the foredeck with every plunge. Gerald was sure he was going to die when this ferry sank. That was the way it would be. But he would face death proudly, feeling like he was flying over the water. When they made it back to St. Ignace, Gerald was cold and soaked through. His teeth were chattering so hard he could hardly speak. "Are you okay?" Howard asked Gerald as they stepped ashore. "I... in... incredible," Gerald stammered. "Amazing," Brian said sarcastically.

◆◆◆

G2 STOOD A LITTLE WAYS OFF from the small group that gathered in the cemetery. It didn't make any difference what city he was in; this ritual took place once a year. Half a dozen preacher-types in the robes of different faiths gathered around a grave as a stone was laid over it. They sang a song G2 didn't know. A man with an ID badge hanging around his neck spoke about the county's responsibility to provide a respectful burial for the indigents who have no family able to care for their remains. This year, over 200 cremated remains were to be added to the vault where hundreds already lay. "We need to take care of our homeless population," said the man with the badge. "Sometimes that includes taking care of their final resting place." A television crew interviewed the man and one of the preachers at the gravesite. There were only a dozen others present by the grave. G2 looked around. The homeless were there. No more than shadows behind a tombstone or a tree, they silently said their goodbyes to family, friends, or acquaintances and then slipped away from the cemetery before anyone noticed them. G2 sat beside a marker that read, "James Martin, devoted husband and father, 1942-2001." *59 years old*, G2 thought. He was nearly that. Almost two thirds of his life had been spent with no place that he called home. James Martin had a home. It was right here in this graveyard. That's what a home was, after all. A graveyard.

Somewhere his father and mother had a home. Maybe other people G2 knew, too. He wondered if in the cemetery the dead ever talked with each other. If so, would James Martin be sauntering over to the indigent grave saying welcome to the neighborhood? Or would he be organizing a committee to get the homeless campsite moved to a different part of the cemetery so the value of his lot didn't go down. Or maybe, James Martin was too busy with playing his harp and shining his halo to notice that 200 more people had just moved into his neighborhood. It seemed there was always room for more.

When the camera crew had left and the preachers were gone, a crew came out and took down the little tent that they'd put up over the site to keep the rain off. G2 was pretty damp by then, but when they left he stumbled over to the marker and read the list of names. He thought he recognized one or two. Didn't know what had happened to Margaret McGwire. Now she rests in peace, better cared for in death than she had been in life. "God bless," G2 whispered and then wandered out toward the highway.

♦♦♦

"IT WAS ONLY A FISH," Gerald's mother said. Nonetheless, she prepared the tiny goldfish respectfully as the children watched. There would be a "burial at sea" she told them. Sparky the goldfish had come to them as part of a children's carnival at school. Gerald still wasn't sure what he had done to "win" the fish. It seemed that everyone who attended had managed the feat, however. He had thrown balls at milk cartons, bean bags through a clown's face, and had skipped, jumped, and hopped over ten feet. Marion had only managed three feet, but she was only three years old. Sparky lived in a quart Mason jar in Gerald's room and he fed the fish generously two or three times a day. In two weeks, the jar was filled with cloudy water and Sparky was listing to one side. His mother used a kitchen strainer to transfer Sparky

123

to a clean jar and water and soaked his former home in dish detergent and hot water for most of a day before she could face putting the bottle brush into the opening. But Sparky had never straightened up and two days later was floating on his back at the top of the jar. His mother had put the fish through the strainer again and set another jar to soak. She dumped the body out onto a piece of toilet paper and rolled it up. "It's a burial shroud," she told the children. Then they marched into the bathroom and she slid Sparky off a wooden spatula into the toilet bowl and flushed. "May Sparky swim in freedom in the underground rivers and sewers from this day forward," his mother intoned as the children stood at attention and saluted.

Gerald had never thought of the notion of underground rivers before. It was cool. If he had his choices, maybe he would be buried at sea as well. He wondered how you would flush a person into the sewers. That must be what they did at the big sewage treatment plant. He imagined a big toilet bowl where his body would go round and round in a circle until it flushed out of sight into the wonderful world of underground rivers to swim there forever. It didn't bother Gerald that poop also got flushed down that hole. After all, it had been a clean bowl when Sparky went down. He was sure there were different passages. For several nights after that, Gerald dreamed of going round and round in circles to the underground rivers to swim there forever. Amen.

♦♦♦

G2 FOUND HIMSELF once again in front of the Manhattan Club. He was pretty sure it was Wednesday, but he hadn't seen the guy. Maybe he was on vacation. It was hot enough, even up north. Maybe he'd gone to the lake and was dragging his kids on skis behind a big powerful boat. G2 knew that was what he'd be doing if he were at the lake this time of year. In fact, he bet he could still find his way up to that lake. What was the name of it, anyway? Something Indian-sounding. He sat there in front of the café and held his sign in front of him. Most everyone ignored him. He didn't care. He had a bottle stashed in his bag and knew he could get a little food from the kitchen if he went around back, even if he had to dumpster dive to get it. The guy would be there. He was as sure of that as that his name was G2. Or Gerald

Good. Whatever. Gerald automatically reached for his pad of paper when he saw the green Toyota pull up to the curb. 666-BST. How could that person drive around in a car that had the mark of the beast on it? It was risking an awful lot. Not that G2 believed in a beast or a mark, but a lot of hobos held the mark in high regard. Putting 666 on a tree or mailbox spoke ill of the family who lived there. They all avoided railcars numbered 666 and G2 had once seen the numbers tagged on the inside of a box car. The car had a foul odor and G2 found a different one to ride in.

He was so intent on analyzing the license plate that he almost missed the guy coming out of the restaurant. He was alone, that was strange. Usually they only came to the Manhattan on business or with friends, but the guy was looking a little tipsy. Must have had a two martini lunch. Maybe three, G2 thought when the guy tripped in front of him and almost fell. His hand snaked out and G2 could see the wadded up dollar bill in his fingers, ready to drop in his cup. But then it happened. The guy didn't let go of the bill. He turned toward it as if it had hold of his hand rather than the other way around. And when he looked at the dollar, he looked at G2. Their eyes locked and G2 could see in them all that he'd missed in life. He could see a wife and family, money, success, a house, community standing. It was all there, right where he'd left it… what? thirty years ago? thirty-five? Forty? It was his. All his. The guy snatched his hand back.

"Let's go get a drink, buddy," he said. The guy waved him along and G2 got up and followed around the corner from the Manhattan Club. They went toward the waterfront and near the ferry terminal the guy led G2 into a bar that was dark. The floor was sticky and G2's feet tore away from it as they walked to a table. They sat down and the guy hollered at the bartender. "Bring this guy a glass of wine and I want a whiskey and water. No. Forget the water." The guy turned and looked at G2. "I'm celebrating," he said. "Celebrating my freedom." They waited until the bartender brought them their drinks and the guy ordered himself another as soon as he had one in hand. "To freedom!" he said as he clinked his glass against G2's. G2 hadn't drunk wine out of a glass in months. And that was a water glass he stole from a shelter. And it was plastic. He picked up the glass and swirled the wine around the edges. *It's got legs,* he thought absently. He took a thoughtful sip and held the wine in his mouth, swished it around and let the feeling of the tanins and oak fill the back of his palette. The bartender set down another whiskey and took the guy's empty away. "We got a God damned connoisseur here," the guy laughed. "This is no wino." They sat for a long time in silence as the guy nursed his second whiskey and G2 took another sip. "You need some food to go with that," the guy said. He hollered at the bar tender again and eventually a pile of French fries showed up at their table. G2 smiled and ate one so fast it burned his mouth and his throat. He had to take another sip of wine to cool it off. Frankly, it wasn't that good a wine. He'd had better out of a three-liter box that he got for fifteen bucks when he was feeling flush once. Boxes were hard to carry in his bag, though, so G2 didn't get them unless he owed a camp boss a round.

"I have been the national salesman of the year fifteen times in the past twenty-five years," the guy said. "That's pretty damn good." He clinked his glass against G2's again. "They're thinking of renaming the God damned award after me when I retire, but I never do. I'll retire someday, I suppose. Till then, they're stuck giving me the damned thing. I got a house out by the water, beautiful view and a whole shelf full of sales awards and recognitions. Cabin up north on Lake Superior, too. Nice car. Two. Expense account. I need an expense account. I'm on the road half the year. So of course, I got a mistress or two tucked away in different cities. Not that they'd miss me, but I'd miss them. Just like I'm going to miss my wife. She left me this morning. Said there wasn't really any sense being married since she never sees me. No hard feelings, but she's moving to Omaha fucking Nebraska to be with her sister. Oh. Not my first wife. She took the kids and left years ago. I never see them. Christmas card in the email. I send them a bunch of money and they don't even call me." They sat in silence again for a few minutes. G2 took another sip of the wine. Well, it wasn't that bad.

"See, the thing is I was like you once. I got a big break and I went out to make something of myself. And by God I did. I'm a successful man. I've got it all. And you know what? I don't fucking care. You could take the whole thing and it wouldn't make a bit of difference to my life. I'd still be a drunk, fast talker, who could sell refrigerators to Eskimos as well as I sell iron to the steel companies. Wouldn't make a bit of difference. It doesn't make you happy. It's a deal with the devil, that's what it is. Barkeep! Whiskey!" the guy waited until the bartender had cleared the glass and checked G2's. The fries were gone, so he took the plate. "I've got a deal for you, mister. I'll give it all to you. Don't worry about not being able to do my job. You don't need it. I got plenty of money, even after the wife gets her share. You take all my money, my house, my car, and my life. I'll take whatever you've got in that bag and you'll never see me again. Deal? I took the deal. You should take the deal." He was silent for a moment and then looked at G2 as if he were stone-cold sober. "I'm serious," he said. "I'll give it all to you. That's how I got started. It's the least I can do for someone else. Maybe then it would all have some kind of meaning. I'd be satisfied that I did something good for somebody. I'd know in my heart it was all worth it. I got a buddy who'll make it all legal and everything. What do you say?"

This was it. G2 to could reclaim all that was his. He thought about Lori. He'd go back to her. He'd go see his sister and find his mother. He'd talk to a publisher about the book he was going to write and all the notes he kept over the past thirty some years. He'd drink good wine again and not whatever rot-gut he could get with a screw top on it. G2 could be Gerald again, take a shower and sleep in clean sheets. He could drive a big car. He'd have an ex-wife or two and a mistress in a couple places where he traveled. First he'd have to get a shower and shave. No. First he'd call his sister. No. First he'd buy a bottle of good wine and celebrate. No. As much as G2 tried to put himself in that life, he couldn't see it. He couldn't even decide what he should do first. He took another sip of wine. It wasn't bad at all. Would he get the mistresses and the ex-wives and the children who never called? He'd go straight up to the lake and drive the ski boat. No. He'd take a long vacation and fly in an airplane to Paris. No. He'd… Maybe he should think this through. He'd never have to ride the rails again — never be able to ride the rails again. Always be in his one house with its roof and its mortgage and the plumbing to get repaired. It would be a home without a headstone. He'd have neighbors he'd talk to.

People would want him to speak at seminars about the homeless. They'd want his advice on how to deal with the problem. G2's heart was beating hard. His mouth was dry and he took another sip of that fine wine, held it in his mouth and let the vapors fill his sinuses and wash down his throat. There was a twitch in the leg that had been wounded once and it beat in time with the clack-clack-clack of the rails as the train went down the track. And the stars. Sure, it would be cold out in the winter, but that's what Florida was for. There was a ringing in G2's ears and through it all he could hear was his own voice as he stood and laid a hand on the guy's shoulder. "I volunteered," he croaked.

G2 turned. He'd just eaten hot greasy French fries and a glass of fine wine. He headed toward the door of the little bar, then turned and bobbed at the man, still sitting with his whiskey glass half way to his mouth. "God bless," G2 said, and left. He wasn't happy or satisfied. But he wasn't sad or depressed either. He was G2, and there really wasn't any sense thinking about anything else.

It was still hot outside. G2 headed for the tracks. A freight was just beginning to move in the yard. G2 sprinted toward a jimmie and caught onto the ladder and jumped into the well He'd have to go south a ways before he could catch a freight train west. He'd see some mountains. He reached for the bottle in his bag and realized that he'd left it in the bar. His heart jumped into his throat and he stood in the hopper well. He could jump and go back to get his bag. But then the train would be gone. He'd have to wait. Maybe he'd reconsider his decision and take the guy up on his offer. The train was picking up speed. There was no sense in going back. It wasn't the last bottle of wine in the world. He'd just ride this train away. That was the thing about trains. They never took you back. They only took you away.